"In such stories as "Panther," "Reptile Man," "The Trouble with Fire," and "Turing Test," the author takes decisive aim at contemporary social media culture and advanced technology; an angel behaving like a stand-up comic surveying the history of humankind speaks of "all the words and noise that interfere with any sense at all." However, Dragan's narrative imagination makes substantial sense of the impact of that interference."

—Thomas Fink, Poet and Literary Critic

"The mood of 'The Builder of Invisible Bridges' is still tinged with melancholy, though—to be expected in any depiction of life in war-torn countries with totalitarian regimes. It's a story about humanity surviving in spite of itself. About the definition of luck when one's fate could always have been worse. And the tender construction of sacrifice and connection, keeping said humanity intact."

—Tom Dooley, editor *Eclectica Magazine*

INVISIBLE BRIDGES

STORIES

INVISIBLE BRIDGES

RICHARD DRAGAN

COMET TAIL PRESS

COMET TAIL PRESS

"Flesh and Blood" was published in *Columbia's Quarto* magazine.

"The Builder of Invisible Bridges" and "Just Out of Reach" were published in
Eclectica Magazine.

"Builder" was selected for its *Best Of Fiction* anthology
and published there: ISBN 978-099688300.

Book cover and interior design by Monkey C Media
monkeyCmedia.com

First Edition
Printed in the United States of America

ISBN (paperback): 979-8-9889125-0-7
ISBN (eBook): 979-8-9889125-1-4

Library of Congress Control Number: 2023920891

For AED and CJD

Contents

Panther

By daylight, you are a creature of digital bliss. You text and tweet, you exist almost entirely within the tiny screen, which delivers its predictable bursts of titillation and pleasing endorphins. Like any novice addict, you continually say you could quit at any time. No one knows if this is true because no has ever succeeded in going back to the old ways. In fact, you are proud that you traffic in beautiful surfaces. Who wouldn't be? It's what you use to make a living, to fall in love, to make connections, a badge of your vividly realized life. You are of the moment, a sleek digital creature muscularly pacing inside his virtual cage. For you, meaning happens in bits and bytes, and increasingly in images. Slowing down time with a clumsy book, for example, is the stuff of a bygone age.

So, you are surprised as anyone at your dream of traveling by train, a vision that arrives one night as unpredictably as a petit mal. It's impossible in the waking world. You're late for an indecipherable rendezvous in an old-fashioned train with brown wooden paneling. Moving from car to car, you search for a seat, but every single one is filled with characters from a traveling circus, a dozen cars now and always the same thing. The harlequins, a clown, two pinheads, their heavy misshapen features frightening in the shadows out there. There are dwarves—scads of them—a dancing bear, and two ringleaders wearing spats and sporting megaphones. Even a lion tamer, who sits Indian style on the floor of one compartment.

Near the middle of the train, in his own car, there's a hungry artist wasting away—once a marquee act—barely discernible now in his pile of matted straw. He's reading from a large leather-bound tome, you notice, written in an ornate script, and he offers to tell you a real story for a few coins—a parable, a fable, something un-inventible, unreal, and fantastically true. You shake your head. It's always this way in dreams, isn't it? You're in a hurry and so far behind. He nods that he understands. He's not upset that you are now part of the modern world. He's through with disappointment and returns to his ascetic reading. It's just possible that he mouths, "Watch out" in a tongue that you don't really speak in the daytime. Still, the meaning of the phrase is successfully conveyed.

The train is moving fast now, its night speed. It's the wee hours, no need to slow down in the small villages across the steppes and the frozen tundra. No chance of hitting an oxcart here or a horse-drawn carriage, much less an automobile. This is that kind of dream where you've been transported to a different, earlier time. Magic and folklore, it seems, will be permitted.

Some kind of intercom calls out your name as you walk through each crowded compartment. Soon, it's all but impossible to make any forward progress at all. There are more and more members of the circus, a traveling carnival really. There's a tightrope walker, a whole family of them, men, women, and small children dressed in matching bright-red leotards, mulling around some kind of pedestal. Each one prances along an improvised tightrope strung between two seats, then balancing and standing curiously on one leg as the train rumbles mightily along. Those old 19th-Century tracks are clumsily laid down. It's a rough ride, but a safe one, as the juggernaut you ride flattens any imperfectly laid iron track. You are amazed that not one of them stumbles or falls.

The train speeds up faster and faster. It's more crowded now, though that isn't possible. You are an obstacle yourself, as men in fedoras carry suitcases stamped with a collage of hotel names in faraway cities indicating a lifetime of traveling sales from all over the world. They're charging through the train, against you in the opposite direction, with a cartoon-like velocity, actually holding onto their hats, almost clobbering you as they jostle by with their bulky steamer trunks crowded with sample articles.

One last time, you cross the deafening threshold between cars. The sound of the train almost deadens as you shut the door behind you. You smell creosote, the heavy sulfur of coal, a notable smell in the icy Siberian air, then welcome warmth and the train's thunder muffled on the other side of the glass. You seem to be safe, though the train's force is still there, pounding behind the thick glass. Now you discern an animal smell, the scent of fresh meat, dung, clotted fur. You can see nothing, it's pitch black almost, but you perceive a muted growl, then a dim green flash of a large feline eye as big as an old Roman coin. Suddenly, you trip forward and reach out into the darkness, grabbing onto anything to break your dream fall. You feel the ice-cold bars of a cage as you grope in the darkness. There he is: sleek, black, his dark outline a more perfect dark than the blackness all around you both. He's pacing back and forth in his cage and doesn't bother to notice you, at least not right away. Why should he? He's confident in his sinew, he could jump and go right through those insubstantial bars. He barely acknowledges you. The green eyes stare at you for a moment—just a half second or two, a semiquaver of time—then he turns to go to the other side of the cage.

It's darker than ever. You feel a hot breath on the back of your hand. It's warm, wet, laden with the smell of his last meal.

How did he get out? Did someone forget to lock his cage? His full face is in front of you. His eyes glow like a canvas out of Rousseau, the one where the viewer and the big cat hypnotize each other. Like a mentalist's trick, neither can move. He's holding your hand in his jaws. It's warm, terrifying, yet you can do nothing else. You're his unexpected prey. Someone is again calling your name out of the darkness now. No, you will never find the diner car for one last pleasant meal. You have been deceived, somehow, as the beast rears up on its hind legs, taking you all at once into his mouth, a crescendo of heart-racing panic. Maybe, just maybe, you should have listened to the teller of tales earlier in the train.

Waking is a relief, but also a loss. Your dog licks your hand in real life, kind enough not to bark. The alarm is off and you're late, very late, and he wants his usual walk and breakfast.

Flesh and Blood

Surely he should have been somewhere else, somewhere less to do with shadows and this business of lurking. That was his job, incessant lurking, dispassionate observation behind the viewfinder, hiding behind the crosshairs in his studio, a loft, actually, that seemed always to fill up with damp as if after a rain. There, Hilmar photographed babies, mothers, brides, grooms, high school debutantes, and cheerleaders, those categories of people most concerned with human feeling, he suspected, which he had thrown aside some years ago for much more private and stringent obsessions.

People came to him for photographs of the dead as well as the newly living. He retouched the images of deceased relatives and friends. Usually, he cropped out the living from the corner and centered the frame around the one who had passed on.

He preferred the old ways. He wanted nothing to do with pixels and data. The photographer turned careless snapshots into icons to treasure, something to hold onto, to place on the mantel over the dull light of a waning fire and to savor in the space of a moment or two before resuming the old battle with everyday noise. He tinted photographs with chemicals so toxic as to eat away the fingertips of the leather driving gloves he wore through an idiosyncratic (so he believed) sense of fashion in the world of the darkroom, the place where he birthed his faces of the missing, who routinely reappeared as if by an austere magic under the stopper bath, still smiling as if nothing were wrong or looking somber and skeptical (he found that many of his subjects who had passed into the beyond had been preserved in moments that intimated their pending demise). These faces kept their expression under the water as he washed them. They seemed quite content to drown.

The daguerreotype portrait that one could hold in the hand, he knew, was invented to remember the dead in a time of disease, medical charlatanism, and ignorance that did little good to anyone. So went the origins of the photographer's art. The image of the dead child in its flowered crypt kept a memory alive, at least until the beholder succumbed to the same war, the same influenza, the same typhus soon after. One could do little except look on and pray.

The photographer considered himself the heir to his art's original intent. Hilmar was a traditionalist. The surveillance outside his studio was a messy extension of his real work back in the dark, but he enjoyed it, too. To be able to walk around in the park with his lenses and measure the world around him in its shadows and raw visual forms, which appealed, he suspected, to the inner core of his brain, the reptilian center most preoccupied with temperature, hunger, crude survival. It was this part of him which caused him to seize certain situations over others within the frame of his lens.

The woman was playing with her leather handbag now as she sat uncomfortably on the metal park bench in a pose of uncomfortable expectation, of waiting for a friend or lover who might not show, half hoping that he wouldn't, in fact, because if he came, there would no doubt be discord. The woman, who was tall and dressed in a red cashmere coat, now examined the back of her hands as though searching them for hints of age. She smirked, unhappy with what she found, though she was perhaps only thirty-five and her dark hair showed no trace of gray. The photographer watched the woman readjust her coat nervously on the surface of the seat. He liked the way her body didn't seem to fit the bench. He took a few shots, the silent shutter of his Leica whirring like a timid night insect out prematurely in the light of afternoon.

The woman's elegance, the set of her attenuated limbs reminded him of a Modigliani or a Mannerist painting, the angular jut of her jaw reminiscent of his very first model, Louisa, whom he met in a bar in Frankfurt during his student days. That night, Louisa had said she was nineteen, but she obviously wasn't, and she'd been extraordinarily drunk. When he took her back to his room at the pension, a little larger than the trunk for his camera equipment, she seemed a willing enough victim. When he asked her to be politely tied up with a variety of ropes and makeshift gags, she wasn't as concerned as he thought she might be. She only laughed a drunk's laugh and abandoned all forms of caution. He had only wanted to photograph her in varying degrees of undress. He had planned no more. When she was free to go, without even a chafed wrist or ankle for the evening's exertions, it was Louisa who had, in fact, seduced him. They had continued to see each other for about six months. By the end, she was comfortable posing for him for hours on end. She didn't seem to mind holding still while he re-loaded his camera, set up his floodlights, and held the camera immobile while coaxing her into the exact position dictated by that inner, lidless eye that told him what he wanted. In those black and white images taken in the chill of winter, Louisa's gooseflesh was visible. Hilmar was pleased with the detail and always felt a pleasing tinge of nostalgia and distinct memory—indeed, much like a photograph—whenever he looked back on his student period.

He had sent Louisa a copy of his first book that featured some of her photographs. Not his best work, he thought, but he had written that he thought she was ravishing. Louisa had written back in her own letter that whenever she thought on their time together, she felt physically cold. He had no idea why.

His new subject hadn't moved for some time. Presently, a balding, short, and squat man wearing a leather coat that extended well past his fat knees now approached the woman on the bench, smiling guilelessly, the smile of an angel. She stood to meet him. The photographs from this moment were taken in rapid succession, with Hilmar's zoom lens turned full up. They showed the woman rear up in her seat as if surprised that it was indeed time to meet the person she had spent nearly an hour anticipating. In the first frames, the woman had put on what looked like a resplendent smile of her own. Only after the first twenty frames did the camera detect that she was terrified; on closer inspection, the smile looked like that of a weirdly happy mannequin. Although Hilmar's photos could only hint at motion, one could imagine that in these middle images, the corners of the woman's thin red lips were quivering at their upturned edges at the impossibility of carrying off her deceit.

The man in the coat now grimaced. He embraced the woman as if administering a kiss of betrayal. He lunged his wide body toward her. She was defenseless at his approach and could only accept the violation of the buffer zone of her private space. This image, one of the best, Hilmar later believed, showed her looking panicked and distant as the man's lips contacted her pale cheek. Perhaps it was the cold, or real fear, but under extreme magnification of the image, one could discern the outline of a welling tear in an eye made dull by terror. As the man retreated, her posture seemed to dissolve; she crumpled noticeably as she stepped back. Then the short man stood with his legs apart, savoring the power of conquest. Here, the photographer switched to his backup camera, having exhausted his first thirty-six exposures and having no time to reload. The new camera, an old Nikon, was bulkier, its black metal body cold to his touch.

The woman and the man, one hundred and fifty feet away and invisible, they believed, to everyone, now exchanged words. The woman reeled back even more, and suddenly, though the open shutter did not capture the impact, let loose a slap that landed on the right side of the man's face. The camera would record only the twist of his neck in reflex to fresh pain and the woman's now genuine smile at her momentary triumph. The man, however, retaliated, and the photographer was actually surprised at the force and suddenness of the man's blow to her head, the way her body flopped sideways to the ground like a child's discarded toy and the man's subsequent solitary and equally vicious kick. The photographer only managed to capture the blurred image of the man's receding frame as he walked rapidly down the path, away from the woman, and the twitches of her legs and arms as she contorted in distress.

Before Hilmar could think about what he was doing, he found himself running down the hillside from his perch behind his rock to assist the woman. In his haste, he almost forgot his camera bag, but the part of his mind most dedicated to habit remembered to sling the bulky case over his shoulder. His two cameras bounced their costly optics against one another before he could slow down and consider what he was about to do. The woman was sitting up, sobbing quietly, nursing her leg and right temple. Before the photographer could reestablish his invisibility, surely this was what all his instincts impelled him to, the woman called out to his back as he took a step away from her, toward his usual, calculated anonymity.

"Please. Help me," she implored. When he turned, he saw her bloodied face with its mask of total bewilderment. Her former elegance was shattered. His first impulse was to grab for his Nikon and obtain a few shots of her contorted frame, which had taken the mottled shadows of the sunlight through the trees. *How interesting*, he thought to himself. He recalled that one of his favorite artists, Rodchenko, had done a series on wounded faces back in the 1930s. *Or was it Kirchner?* Hilmar continued to speculate. But he was soon watching his hand reach down to the woman, carefully helping her to her feet. Her stocking was torn, and as she stood, she re-established contact with the earth tentatively, like some newly born animal uncertain that legs were in fact designed for supporting the entire weight of the body.

"There you go," he offered as the woman collapsed back onto her bench. Her head was bent to one side as if she were having difficulty with balance. Her left shoe was off, he noticed, as she rubbed a bruised shin with the back of a beautiful hand.

"Thank you," she said. He could tell that if he left now she would probably be too disoriented to remember that she had been abandoned. He could retreat to his room and work on printing some of the shots of the day. He had the inklings that he had stolen something remarkable from the world today, the worth of which could perhaps only be savored back in his dark lair.

The photographer wasn't sure of what to say. He was surely more visual than verbal. And now nothing was clear to him.

"Do you want the police?" he asked, really not sure of whether she would want to involve the authorities because of the suspicious nature of her assailant.

"Later. Perhaps," she said. "Thank you for stopping," she added. She was regaining her composure. He noticed her body had pulled its weight into its previous configuration on the bench. She winced as she rubbed her leg again, her head nodding hypnotically as if acceding to an unstated question only she could hear.

"I was just passing," he replied. "On my way to conduct some business," he continued, motioning to the equipment around his neck.

The woman nodded, as if understanding exactly what his business would be. He knew right then that she was someone of great personal acumen and cunning. He knew from the way her aura reassembled itself. In a few moments, he would not be able to get away. She would be conscious of him, and more importantly, of herself. The chance to walk away and disappear would be lost. He would have to provide his name and other personal, and therefore, incriminating data.

"Not everyone would be as concerned as you," she continued.

"No," he agreed. "I mean, yes, that is unfortunately true."

"My name is Cassandra Klimt," she offered, "I do not, of course, know who you are."

The photographer winced at the implicit suggestion. He looked in the woman's eyes and admired their determination at not letting her pain escape. He felt drawn to them and unconsciously fingered the buttons of his Nikon.

"I'm Hilmar. A photographer," he replied after a pause.

"Thank you, Hilmar," she said, testing out his new name. She was clearly still in pain. He could tell from the way her eyes wanted to glaze over with tears, but her sense of discipline kept her from breaking down.

"Can I take your picture, Ms. Klimt?" Hilmar ventured.

"Mrs. Klimt," she corrected him. "I'm afraid today I am a victim of my ex-husband, whom you have almost had the opportunity to meet."

Yet the woman agreed to his request as though it were totally natural. She only straightened her hair with her finger. She proffered the cut side of her head for the camera. On the black and white film, the smudge of blood on her cheek would perhaps be even more dramatic, despite the loss of color. Hilmar moved quickly, as if guilty about what he was sampling. Even he couldn't have staged the events of the day any better.

"Thank you, Mrs. Klimt," he offered. He was genuinely grateful.

His heart palpitated in his chest as it always did when he had committed a photographic crime of such intensity. On a whim prompted by that darkest part of his brain, the one that understood shapes rather than names, he took her hand and kissed it dramatically, with great compassion and empathy.

Her face registered extreme shock, as if hit by another punch, and then a sublime understanding at Hilmar's extreme gesture of emotional affectation.

"Hilmar," she said, "I don't know what to say."

"Let us go to the police," he petitioned. "Whoever did this to you must be punished."

"I am afraid that the police will not be able to help."

"Whatever you wish," Hilmar said. He suspected that she knew what she was about.

"My ex-husband is a desperately sick man," she went on. "I'm afraid he enjoys expressing himself through violence."

Hilmar nodded his assent. He knew exactly what she meant.

"So it was him. He did this?" Hilmar ventured. He thought it really didn't matter, except for his own curiosity to know the circumstances surrounding his work.

"We met to discuss some money he owes me," she said. "I told him he could surrender it politely or my attorneys would get it from him through legal force." She rubbed her left eye, which was growing bluer as her injury took on a bold, visual form. Once again, Hilmar was possessed by the deep urge to affix the shape of her damaged face to film. He shook his head noticeably at the thought.

"I see that you understand," Cassandra said. "He resorted to calling me names I do not deserve to hear."

She stared off into the trees beyond her, appearing still on the verge of semi-consciousness.

"I had forgotten how hard Georgie can hit, and his ability to sink to great depths."

Hilmar asked what she meant.

"He said he would undoubtedly kill me." She spoke as if reading a fact in a newspaper, staring out past the view, into memory. It was clear that she either didn't comprehend what she was saying or chose not to believe it. Perhaps she was so secretly afraid that she couldn't look at him and tell the stark facts.

"He said tonight everything would be settled."

Hilmar was enchanted. He tried to appear unconcerned. The edge of a plan formed in the blackest root of his brain stem, but he didn't dare bring it up from the dim swamp from which it evolved.

"We cannot let that happen," Hilmar suggested. "I will not let it."

He was clutching onto his camera. Its metal body now warm against his chest. He felt unreasonably confident, slightly invincible.

"Don't worry about me," Cassandra said. "I can take care of myself." There was a pause as she took stock of her situation. "And I hardly even know you," she added. Her eyes had widened and revealed their black centers, liquid and whorling with fear. Hilmar had only seen such a look on his subjects who in real life no longer existed except on the print he was grappling with under his fingers, rinsing it or submerging it into chemicals to attempt to bring that person back to life for someone left behind. Hilmar thought she could be one of his best subjects.

Despite her polite protests, he rode with her in the taxi. She lived on the third floor of an old brownstone made out of mauve brick with white marble ornaments. Sneering gargoyles and child angels lined the top of her roof, guarding her castle from the city below. Hilmar took a few shots of the architecture and the street for documentation. He helped her up the stairs and into the elevator. Her foot was still giving her keen discomfort. Her left calf had purpled and was markedly swollen. Her head was still set on the rest of her body incorrectly; it listed noticeably whenever she attempted to walk on her own. Still, Cassandra's fundamental dignity, her will not to appear vulnerable, was intact. Hilmar was quite impressed with her bearing.

Out of reluctance or dizziness, she hesitated while searching for her key in her handbag. Hilmar persisted, however, feigning chivalry and empathy—though there was a touch of this to be sure. He was most interested in making sure she was safely ensconced in her apartment. Then he could go on with his other plans.

The apartment itself was palatial. It must have occupied the whole floor and some additional heretofore undiscovered space in the building. It was an architect's playground: sleek metal-framed furniture set at well-considered intervals in the main room. There was a white leather ottoman, a rug of some kind of striped skin on the floor, and huge windows that looked over a tiny garden and then the profile of the entire city. He sat Cassandra down; her sleek lines complemented those of the chair, he thought, and he fought off a subterranean impulse to ask her to tilt her head to one side into a beam of light given off by a lamp in the corner. But he had packed his cameras away on the ride over.

"You must go to the hospital," he reminded her. "As you promised."

"I'll see my doctor tomorrow," she said. "I'll be perfectly fine in the morning."

The photographer didn't think so. He was convinced that Cassandra had some kind of mild concussion.

"Fewer questions," she explained. "My physician has seen this thing with me before. I don't have to invent anything, like falling down the stairs."

Hilmar was touched by her revelation. He was convinced that this Georgie was even more monstrous than she had described. From the first day of their time together, he had been violent. Apparently, he was an unscrupulous importer; he brought cheese, rugs, and even illegal ivory into the country. He wasn't a gangster himself, Cassandra said, but he worked with gangsters every day, and the petty criminals of many lands. His work took him to many different countries, where he made all kinds of money, she said. Georgie had been prodigiously unfaithful to her, yet he had always made up for it, even after the occasional excla-mations of violence, with exquisite gifts: paintings, jewels, poems of his own devising, written on the jet between Hong Kong and Los Angeles. It wasn't the money that held her in his grasp; she had enough of that on her own. It was something inside her, she was convinced, that was bent on something close to self-annihilation that had kept her with Georgie for almost four years.

Hilmar listened to her story intently, as if conducting a psychological interview, an assessment, an initial and important observation that would determine the course of treatment for this patient now supine on the couch. He told her that he understood everything, that she needed rest most of all, and that he would be back to check on her later.

"I need to take care of some personal affairs," he told her. He could tell that she was skeptical of his intentions but that she knew that if she had trusted him so far, there wasn't enough evidence to shift her alliance, to tell herself to act on her own. He also noticed that she seemed very tired. He poured her a tall glass of gin mixed with some orange juice that he found in her refrigerator, careful to wipe the bottle and glass after he was finished pouring. He watched her sip it slowly and methodically, then she collapsed once more on the couch and fell asleep. Hilmar took some liberties with his lens this time, convinced that he had full license. He photographed her torn stocking. He photographed her chest uneasily rising and falling. He photographed the lie of her hair on her velour throw pillow, and then he found himself out of film. Before he left, he fished the keys out of her handbag. He turned out the lights with his elbow and made sure the door was locked. Once he was convinced that Cassandra was in no pressing danger, he walked out of the apartment, the click of his heels echoing emptily on the marble floor of the lobby. He turned into the fading day and planned on what equipment he would need later that evening.

***

At nine o'clock, Hilmar knocked on the door, not loudly enough to wake her should she be at home and still sleeping. He carried a bulky bag over his shoulder, which contained some necessary tools: a few lights, a collapsible tripod, and two dozen rolls of film. He was wearing a pair of driving gloves that he used in his darkroom. He didn't want, of course, to leave anything as personal as fingerprints. After knocking more loudly and getting no answer, the photographer was convinced that she was either still lost in sleep or missing from the apartment (perhaps she had taken herself to the hospital, after all, Hilmar thought).

He opened the door with guarded suspicion and peered into the dim outlines within the huge nave of the apartment. There were no lights on inside, only the hundreds of tiny illuminations from the city's nightscape casting a murky glow into the room from the bay window, adding up to a shade of light just dimmer than a faint moon. Hilmar put his bag next to the door as it closed behind him. He was acutely conscious of the air flowing in and out of his lungs. Though he certainly had four churning chambers inside his chest, he was struck with the feeling that his heart had suspended operation. He imagined his body absorbing the dark air directly like an animal so elemental, so primitive, that it hadn't even developed the need for blood. There in the dark, searching for organic shapes in the corners of the room, shapes that at this moment might present danger, Hilmar felt that he was his own creator. He now had his camera in one hand and his other ready to defend himself.

Cassandra lay unconscious in a heap in the kitchen underneath a glass table. Her eyes were half open. They fluttered slightly as she breathed. Her limbs were folded underneath her as though sleeping. Before attending to her, Hilmar checked the rest of the apartment for other signs of life. He found nothing. He called out her name, but there was no motion. He then touched her cheek and found that it held an odd chill. He picked her up and carried her to the couch. She was very heavy. Through his exertions, he felt the blood returning to his hands and feet. He felt the regular pattern of his heartbeat through his black shirt. Cassandra stirred as she was being dropped back on the cushions. Her breathing was irregular, an uneven rasp. Hilmar began dialing for an ambulance, then he put the phone back in its resting place. Someone was scratching at the door, fumbling with keys. He turned around just as a band of light from the hall carved a dim trapezoid out of the blackness of the room. It was Georgie, earlier than expected, wearing what looked like a ski mask. His wide body was dressed completely in black. He hesitated before he put his foot through the doorframe. But he must have not noticed Hilmar or

Cassandra at first because he walked into the room with the uncareful swagger that had made an impression on Hilmar from the experience of the afternoon.

"Cassie? Cassie!" said Georgie in the darkness. His voice was quiet and gruff. It promised unlimited malice. He didn't seem to be carrying a weapon, but Hilmar suspected from Cassandra's description that Georgie would be quite content to do his work with only his bare hands.

Hilmar hadn't expected such a direct confrontation. He had expected to set up surveillance in an adjacent room, to assemble the lights and the camera on its tripod for the precise, opportune moment. Despite the change in procedure, Hilmar's reaction was swift, sure, and only appeared to be premeditated. Looking back, he would have said that he had acted upon some vital, instinctual impulse, and that it was exactly this drive that made the photographer what he was.

The photos from these few seconds were not beautiful, Hilmar would be forced to admit. They were shot with an extremely brilliant flash, too bright to preserve the details of the subject under scrutiny, but on the other hand, appropriate to the situation, given the subsequent effects. The images were taken rapidly, with the aid of film ripped through the abdomen of the camera by a motor. They occur every half second, conceived in an intense light much more sterile than sunlight and much more short-lived. There were thirty-six of them. They showed a hooded figure in a mask with a wrestler's compact frame stopped abruptly from its tentative, forward motion through the door. They showed a hand sprouting hairy knuckles reaching behind the back of the head as if for a secret resource, a concealed weapon. But what is revealed is a middle-aged man's thinning hairline, eyes that are round with shock, large jowls, and a menacing expression about the lips. The precise detail of Georgie's face came back to Hilmar even in those fragile seconds in the darkness, exploded by these small strokes of lightning. Under more serene conditions, Hilmar would have liked to shoot Georgie more carefully. He had a visually intriguing face, at once exquisitely padded with flesh, and undoubtedly grotesque like an overweight bulldog. Hilmer's visual lobe in his brain had to agree, despite any misgivings about Georgie's personal character. The middle ten frames showed this grappler put up his guard and reached into his pocket. There were two or three frames where the subject was clearly searching for something that didn't exist. One could tell by the look of desperation that came across the heavy face. Perhaps, Hilmar later thought, Georgie was used to carrying a gun, but for this job, which satisfied such personal needs, he had decided against it and opted for a more brutal and bare-knuckled technique.

The latter half of the series—which weren't quite in focus because the subject under surveillance had moved too quickly for the auto-focus to compensate—showed Georgie turning as if to begin a sprint and pouncing back through the doorframe, like some large bear or buffalo suddenly wounded, hurt, desperate for open spaces where it could recuperate in quiet. The camera could not record it, of course, but Hilmar heard Georgie's deep growls as he made his way to freedom.

When Georgie was gone, Hilmar found his newly-returned heart palpitating, not out of fear as much as the excitement, the adrenaline rush of what was captured and would be transferred from one darkness to another, from that of the inside of the camera underneath his trembling fingers to that of his black room at home.

After checking the hallway and closing the door, Hilmar dialed an ambulance for Cassandra, who seemed to be sleeping better now. The photographer reloaded his Leica and took another few shots of Cassandra's slumbering form. He couldn't wait for the ambulance to come. There would be too many questions to answer. There was always that camera obscura of memory, which filled in details with extraneous—and artificial—material. It distorted and denied whatever it wanted, he knew. But Hilmar had saved the real facts, the absolute story for later, which could be exposed privately in all its luxuriant detail in the comfort of his studio as a sequence of preciously paid-for images. To his mind, that truth was perfect and could not ever be taken away.

Reptile Man

Every day there are more and more crocodiles in Mrs. Samuel's backyard, their warted and gleaming green bodies enclosed by her white picket fence. They congregate around the bird feeder, waiting for robins, for jays, for starlings. They sun themselves contentedly like Buddhas, yawning between meals. There's really nothing she can do about them.

Widowed Mrs. Samuel, with her bucket and jogging shoes, walks out every morning, surprised each day by their growing numbers. She's there at six A.M. at the latest to feed them bread crusts and table scraps, chicken or soup bones, slabs of old meatloaf, apple peels, paper plates soaked through with chicken fat, or pork rinds. It's not that Mrs. Samuel considers herself generous. It's just that she finds that she cooks too much for herself lately, and she has never been one to tolerate waste. So, there she is every morning, with her self-imposed regimen. She stands carefully with her white plastic bucket, balancing on an old redwood bench, which allows her to reach over her side of the fence.

Here they come, she imagines, the crocodile families, the crocodile brothers and sisters, the mother and fathers, running, sidling, with their eager, writhing bodies that are so agile when they need to be, toward her, as if summoned to a picnic.

Once they approach the hand of Mrs. Samuel, they are patient (they are well-trained by now) and don't open their mouths until she lowers a handful of food down to them in order—these are suburban reptiles, after all. One by one they approach her, as if to take communion, she imagines, and they crack open their immense jaws, showing rows and rows of fearsome yellow teeth. Mrs. Samuel places a bone or a chunk of gristle or other morsel in the middle of their fat, pink tongues. There is a snap of teeth for some of the more aggressive specimens, but most of the crocodiles will hold their dinner in their mouths as if waiting for a signal, and then, after swallowing, take their place at the end of the line.

They are greedy, most of them, even if they are polite. At first, there were seconds and even thirds. Now they are fortunate to be fed once, now that there are so many of them. Their order threatens to break down, Mrs. Samuel fears. Is it possible, she asks herself, that after feeding, one or two of them wave their green tails in contentment, one or two swipes of crocodile flesh, like overgrazed cows?

Mrs. Samuel goes about her simple business. She has found she doesn't mind not seeing people anymore. Since her best friend Ollie disappeared during the Florida winter, the rainy season, she has found a reserve of strength she didn't know existed. After he walked right into the bayou, into swampy oblivion, she hasn't missed him as much as she imagined she would. She spends her time at the public library or on her verandah, reading and thinking. And every morning, so bright and early, dressed in her brown print dress, her thick, sturdy ankles balancing her frame, she bends over her fence into the backyard to feed her charges. She's getting a reputation as quite an eccentric in the neighborhood, but when she thinks about how much those creatures need her, have grown to depend on her, and perhaps love her, she doesn't mind. Let people think what they want, she tells herself. She has necessary responsibilities to the reptile kingdom.

***

She thinks of Ollie, the reptile man (it was true, he had taken a college course in paleo anatomy), on one of her pilgrimages to the natural history museum near the university. He was always someone caught in the past, admiring the skeletal record of geologic time when lizards as large as apartment buildings roamed a world covered with swamp and sea. There'd been something truly sad in Ollie's last days. He had lost his job at the museum, a place he so dearly loved. Often, he would spend the night working among the hulking dinosaur shadows that filled the nave of the main room of the museum. He had invited her along sometimes. He would tell her stories of his work, about reptile eating habits, their wants and desires, their distinctive way of walking the earth, their breeding habits and struggle to exist in a world that ceased to want them, favoring warm-blooded, smaller, and faster creatures instead.

Mrs. Samuel had gained an appreciation for Ollie in those moments that she never could muster when they were at home in front of the television. When he looked out past his heavy- framed glasses, his eyes compressed behind unbelievably thick lenses, she knew that she really loved him. When he took a moment to scratch his balding head or his thick white beard to explicate some finer point of reptile anatomy, she nodded her head as though she were one of his children to whom he gave tours of the museum. He explained that most of the skeletons in the room were sculpted largely out of plaster. There were three of them with their tremendous skulls and vertebrae and limbs. Often, there weren't enough bones to go on, Ollie said, and it was his job to reconstruct them using his know-how and precise sculpture's eye for ancient anatomy.

He had taken her into the back rooms of the museum where there were rows and rows of plaster dinosaur bones laid out side by side on large tables. Each one was cast by hand, by Ollie and the other workers. After each component had been carefully molded, they would be assembled using metal tubing and wire. The skeleton would be resurrected right under their hands. Ollie had promised that Mrs. Samuel could watch one day as they did this. But he didn't think they would appreciate an outsider in the museum's dinosaur factory. Reptile men were strange characters, Ollie said to her, laughing, making a small circle with a fat finger next to his ear and turning his bald head quizzically. They had trouble relating their great understanding of what was extinct to outsiders. Instead, he said, Mrs. Samuel would have to content herself with examining a partially constructed Stegosaurus, for instance, with only its four feet being builtup on a pedestal. She could easily imagine the rest. She had a gift for filling in the missing pieces. One of the other creatures under construction started with the jaws and neck of a small cousin to the Tyrannosaurus rex—she had forgotten its name by now—and Mrs. Samuel could well imagine the rest of this animal in all its fearful proportions. Ollie explained with a histrionic wave of a pudgy hand that the assembled dinosaurs would be shipped all over the world, to museums, to paleo archeology departments at universities, even to private collectors. Mrs. Samuel, who had only traveled a little bit in the United States, nodded her head in appreciation at the importance of her friend's work. She would, at dangerous moments like these, allow her friend a chance to kiss her on the cheek, or if the mood were right, on the lips. On nights like these, in the main room of the museum in its almost primeval darkness, the two of them held each other carefully, as if they too were made of fragile bones, right under the three, large, sculpted skeletons.

***

But in the end, Mrs. Samuel remembers now, sipping coffee out on her porch, Ollie's perfect station in life had come to a finish. The climate had turned, he said, against the reptile men. He had been visibly weeping that evening as he sat on the empty seat across from her. She recalled a little guiltily that she had laced both their coffees that night with a little rum, though Ollie was certainly a gifted conversationalist without it from all his public tours with all the children at the museum.

The new trend, he'd said, holding back a tearful gasp or two, was that museums wanted machines nowadays. There was a museum in Germany that had done it first, he said, by teaming reptile men with engineers.

"Reptile men are not engineers," Ollie exclaimed. "Engineers have no sense of the poetry, of the art of reconstructing the past from its fossil record," Ollie went on wildly while slamming his mug of coffee on the table so the rum-spiked coffee spilled over.

What had happened, he said, was that the engineers got together and raided the minds of the reptile men. They measured the bones, alright. They brandished micrometers and expressed a concern for suitable precision. But only to get the necessary range of motion for the hip joints, the elbows, the ways the muscles of the dinosaur predators worked their terrible jaws when feeding on prey. The engineers would take their measurements back to their computers, their machine shops, and work only with their sense of unerring accuracy, without any regard for the real facts of the skeleton or for the creative sense possessed by every reptile man—that feeling of the warm plaster under the fingertips was molded just right. Instead, all that knowledge of solid form was discarded, and the German engineers had built out of metal and hydraulics a dinosaur machine, a robot that worked its jaws and swiveled its neck back and forth on a kind of stage, insultingly adding an appropriate soundtrack that suggested a dinosaur roar.

Of course, standards being what they were, Ollie had said, it was irresistible theater. "Audiences, especially children, love to be frightened by a real, live predatory dinosaur," he said. Here he paused and thought a bit to himself. He glanced up at Mrs. Samuel, who looked back at him with wide, patient eyes. "There is no longer any imagination," he said, shaking his head sadly. "The audience might as well be watching a movie."

After hearing Ollie's story, Mrs. Samuel found that she was fighting back a tear or two. Ollie was muttering to himself now. She had to look hard to see his eyes, which were so small behind his glasses, but they had a desperate expression, she thought, which seemed somehow irrevocable. The reptile man, she thought to herself, was no doubt endangered himself.

Orders were pouring in from all over the world, Ollie said, to the German museum, which had found it necessary to form a new corporation, which built a large, automated factory to keep up with the now incessant demand.

"Museums are selling off their skeletons, I'm afraid," he said. "There have been cases, even, where dinosaur skeletons—the ones without any fossil bones at all—have been destroyed," Ollie stated. With explosives, he had heard, the plaster filling the air as men in dust masks reduced the once-majestic outline of a beast to rubble.

"My days all have numbers," Ollie had concluded. He was certain that his section of the museum would go out of business. Already there had been scaled back production and talk of layoffs and rumors that the museum at the university had sent a team to Germany to see the new factory, and to other museums across the country that already had the new and terrible machines, to assess the audience's reactions.

"And what's an old reptile man to do?" Ollie asked. He looked out blankly onto Mrs. Samuel's backyard, into the Florida night, into the swamplands behind her.

That evening, being a person of compassion, and admiring Ollie's courage in the face of his difficulty, she let him stay in her house. They fell asleep holding hands, still dressed, on her twin-sized bed. Ollie said he could take the day off and they could spend it in the park. He said he wouldn't be missed much now that things were so slow at the museum.

***

One morning in spring, Mrs. Samuel goes out to her backyard for her usual duty, and she remembers the night the police called her about Ollie. He was last seen walking along the highway into the untamed swamp. They said that he had been reported missing by his landlady after losing his job. The other men at the museum had said that he had seemed despondent, though there had been no note in his apartment, no indication that Ollie was considering anything drastic. The police had found Mrs. Samuel's number among Ollie's possessions.

The police were treating the situation as a case of missing persons at that point, but they suspected suicide. They told Mrs. Samuel that if she heard anything, anything at all concerning Ollie, that she should contact them immediately. She nodded her assent, of course. She was, at that moment, not really surprised at the news. Ollie had mentioned that he wanted to escape his current situation, that except for Mrs. Samuel (she was flattered when she thought on this), everyone seemed to have it in for the failing reptile man. His few remaining co-workers seemed only to anger him. His landlady, the news on television, the recent decisions for new acquisitions at the museum, it all drove Ollie to the point where he had to take time off, he said. Mrs. Samuel first suspected that he would do some field research in some wetland or jungle or other snaky region of the world. He might go to Africa to study fossils there, or to Malaysia to study Komodo dragons, anything, she suspected, to get away from his current life.

Every day thereafter, she checked her mailbox for a postcard from Ollie, expecting to hear that he was now living in an exotic location.

She hadn't expected the police to come back, but when they did, when they asked whether she could please identify his possessions, she was, at first, absolutely numb. Ollie's wallet and suitcase had been discovered in the bayou by fishermen. It appeared that he had drowned, and after two days of dredging, they had their body, their physical proof. The fishermen had found Ollie's leather wallet and personal belongings, a few books on animal anatomy, some clothing, and an appointment book with Mrs. Samuel's name and number in it. It angered and saddened her even now to think about it. Perhaps he had decided on the local Reptilia as a source of study. Perhaps he had wanted to set up camp right there for a while, only ten miles away, and was caught unaware as he accidentally dozed off.

When they told her the news, Mrs. Samuel stood and nodded and tried not to cry in front of these two strange men with their blue uniforms and official paraphernalia, with their calculated solemnity and stiff expressions on their mouths as they told her, quite matter-of-factly, that her Ollie was dead. She spent the next two weeks inside her house, crying much of the time. Her sadness was of a general kind, and even when she thought about it now, his end made no sense to her. Above her sense of loss was the feeling that somebody else was responsible for his death, not Ollie, certainly. The whole climate of taste had turned against him.

Gradually, her natural sense of resolve took over. Her anger tempered itself into a kind of plan. She thought of ways to change a world that was hostile to reptile men. With a scientist's mind, she worked toward a solution.

She had heard Ollie talk about the generally agreeable nature of the American alligator—that, yes, there were a few attacks on people but nothing like the Egyptian caiman, for example, which sometimes learned to hunt humans as a source of nutrition. But now, Mrs. Samuel imagines that her well-behaved crocodiles are not really all that friendly. She imagines that she has been somehow betrayed, that a betrayal was being planned right before her as she feeds her charges.

A few crocodiles, she imagines this particular morning, the younger, ambitious ones in particular, seem to eye her stumpy legs through the slats in the white picket. They seem to eye her calves with a yearning and a desire that is almost touching to her because it's so impossible, not unless the crocodiles can make themselves so thin, so slight as to crawl under or between the small distance between each slat in the fence. Mrs. Samuel reassures herself that, no, this could never happen. But maybe it's possible that the crocodiles could work together to build some kind of tower of earth shoveled around by their great tails, the same tails, as Ollie once said, that they use to build a nest for their young. No particular crocodiles have yet to raise a family within the four walls of their enclosure here. Her crocodiles just appear as if in a very vivid dream that one can't seem to shake in the daylight. With such a pile of earth, a crocodile Tower of Babel, they might easily climb over to her.

Or perhaps, and this is even more disturbing to Mrs. Samuel as she approaches the fence for the ritual feeding, perhaps they could work together—to climb on top of one another like nervous, overweight cheerleaders, build a pyramid of crocodiles, the most massive crocodiles forming the base for a solid, architectonic structure, the middling-sized ones in the center two or three across, and then the youngest, uppermost crocodiles, who then could be thrown or dropped with a sudden shift of weight onto the unsuspecting Mrs. Samuel.

Or maybe the crocodiles could form a crocodile catapult, again forming some kind of structure with their bodies, two large tails placed side-by-side and with one tremendous and well-calculated heave, they could launch one of the most delicate crocodiles to a sufficient height, flying end-over-end like a discarded valise flung out a window, and onto her as she approached from the other side of the white picket fence.

No, she tells herself, her crocodiles are not that devious. They aren't that clever, she reassures herself. But as she looks at the jaws of one of the largest crocodiles as it gulps up a bone with mechanical precision, Mrs. Samuel is reminded of Ollie and his impulse to escape his machines. She dumps out the remainder of her scraps from the large plastic bucket and walks briskly back to the house. She no longer feeds her pets by hand, of course. How careless she once was, she scolds herself. She hadn't realized the hazard then. Now she feels she is more aware of her surroundings, its unseen danger and quiet conspiracy. She feels capable of genuine action now, and less needful of tears too, though she still sobs a bit now and then on the couch inside her house. She's the only one left, she reminds herself, who understands, and it's up to her to remember something of him, to record what he was about. She thinks about Ollie and his small and knowing eyes that she will never see again. She wants to make sure everyone knows what he stood for.

***

It's Sunday now, and the floor of the museum is dappled with summer sun through its glass ceiling, which plays on the heads of the crowd below. Mrs. Samuel has arrived early to get in position to watch all the people gather. She places her shopping bag next to her along the right edge of the red velveteen ropes that separate the crowd from the newest addition to the museum. The small children cling to their parents in fear. The younger ones bounce up and down in anticipation as they leap across the sunlit floor toward the growing crowd. The parents, even the weary ones, who certainly wouldn't come to the museum unless their children begged after seeing the TV ads, even they pick up their step unconsciously, Mrs. Samuel notices, the crowd rubbernecking to discover what the promised attraction is. This, they tell themselves, is going to be good. Mrs. Samuel, however, is sickened at the cheap theatrics of the new monster, this robotic Tyrannosaurus rex, the king of the dinosaurs, which rears its ugly head and roars so calculatingly. Mrs. Samuel has to admit, however, that its movement seems perfectly natural. Those German engineers, or whoever is responsible for this, have done a good job.

The monster rises twenty-two feet into the air. It swivels its head to-and-fro, roaring spasmodically. A small girl cries out in happiness as the robot's eyes glow brightly. The mob of onlookers is hypno-tized by the effect, which is not so much like a movie but more of a discovery of a living and breathing elephant on safari, Mrs. Samuel imagines. For these people, it's like pushing through the African brush and coming upon a bull elephant rearing its head and trumpeting, its dirty ivory tusks sabering the air, calling the other elephants to battle, to the defense of the herd against some threat, a predator, a group of hunters perhaps. That thrill, which is short-lived yet addictive, is what the crowd first feels. Even Mrs. Samuel must resist the impulse to move closer. She considers, even, that this isn't such a bad occasion after all.

The unveiling is a debut of a new era in museums, when this feeling—this marvelous feeling toward other creatures so much more immense than oneself—can be transported from the primordial jungle and placed here, in public view, where it seems to live and breathe and roar so impressively. How stale, she catches herself thinking, the silent skeleton of the plant-eater—the diplosaurus?—seems in its empty, far north corner of the museum. The board of trustees has decided, the pamphlet in her pocket says, to replace its three sets of bones one at a time with the new technology. So the poor, silent skeleton in the corner doesn't have long to suffer, she thinks. It has become, well, a dinosaur, she realizes.

But even now, the crowd is noticing the cheap latex surface of the monster, its Hollywood paint job, authentic, sure, the pamphlet says, in the style of the Paleozoic reptile, but somehow unimpressive and contrived. The children cannot possibly imagine the pulse of the reptile flesh with every stroke of the great, cold-blooded heart, can they? Or the quivering and ravenous jaws, the stuff of nightmare and imagina-tion? Ollie would say that his skeletons, with their suggestive simplicity, could invite such speculation. The children fill in the gaps, she remembers him saying, and they terrify themselves doing it! There is also that reminder with skeletons, Ollie said once, that our species might just as well be extinct. These new machines will always be fleshed-out, extant, a reminder of our ability to build new, impressive things. "Is that what we're going to teach them, then?" he once asked her. She's not sure that he was right, exactly, but the children even now are beginning to lose interest after their initial thrill. She hears one boy comparing the robot with his favorite cartoon. Another child notices that there are wires concealed under some kind of tape running in the back of the great green tail, which shifts back and forth in the opposite direction of the machine's head.

It seems to be true: most of the children are growing bored. Mrs. Samuel is somehow relieved. She thinks Ollie would be, too. But the sight of the ugly, mechanical beast in its repetitive and threatening pose brings up from within Mrs. Samuel an equivalent response. It evokes from her a protective urge, that somehow, if this monster were not here, she would be with Ollie right now. That if this machine hadn't replaced him, she would have him to talk to at this very moment and they could discuss the imperfections of this calculated spectacle in front of her.

But, of course, this is impossible, and Mrs. Samuel reaches into her shopping bag, the breath caught in her throat at what she is about to do, and she pulls up the small but sturdy sledgehammer that she has been carrying around since this morning. She's been practicing breaking stones, in fact, on her patio. She's always prided herself that she's no slouch when it comes to physical fitness.

She moves with the grace of a boxer as she ducks under the ropes that separate the people from the danger within. She has the feeling of inevitability, that she is carrying out a task that is older than Ollie's fossils, that, yes, this somehow feels right. She barely notes the surprised looks on the faces of the children. *Daddy, what is that lady doing? Will she be safe, Daddy? Daddy!* She doesn't stop to notice the anger and shock register on the faces of the parents who think to themselves, *What is that heavyset woman going to do with that hammer?*

Mrs. Samuel walks right up to the front claw of the monster—who doesn't seem to notice either, of course, its head just keeps lolling away to-and-fro (though its roar is still disconcerting). She knows that she'll get one, maybe two blows at most before the security guards or a few conscientious adults nab her from behind. She winds up just the way Ollie showed her when she was chopping wood once—let the tool's weight do the work—and whirls the hammer over her head, straining her shoulders and thick forearms and bringing the hammer down as a child lets out a scream. She swings so hard that she lets go of the hammer at impact. The heavy tool cleaves into the soft rubber skin of the monster, which parts naturally, giving way to the metal underpinning, its skeleton.

"Now we'll find out what you're really made of!" she says.

The right leg of the monster crumples magnificently as Mrs. Samuel's sledgehammer finishes its downward trajectory. There is spurting of oil and the sizzle of errant electricity as some critical hydraulic tubing gives out. The crowd is silent suddenly as the whole mountain of robotics, rubber, and metal shifts on its base. People step back quickly, there are shouts, and little children are carried to safety by terrified parents.

The fearsome T. rex now teeters in mid-air. It's tied by cables to the wall and ceiling, of course, for just such emergencies, but one of them dislodges from the side of the beast and snaps dangerously back to its mooring on the south wall. Mrs. Samuel smiles when she sees this, because she knows enough about physics to understand that the whole structure is too top-heavy to stand on its own. All those gears and gizmos in the creature's head have made its center of gravity much too high, something the German engineers hadn't anticipated.

As Mrs. Samuel is grabbed by two men in uniform and pulled back to a safe distance, the injured monster lets out a last roar before it reels forward with surprising velocity and at an unexpectedly sharp angle so that its open jaws meet the tiled floor head-on. There is a crunch of muffled impact and the sound of wrenching metal as the giant's tail rips open from behind. It was attached somewhere to the floor, and when it tears open, its inner workings under the thick skin are exposed for all to see. The trunk of the robot somersaults forward to a resting place just inside the red ropes as if its threatening pose were all show anyway and the monster still unable to cross even this most genteel of boundaries.

The soundtrack roar keeps up weakly, though the broken jaws no longer move. The collapsed animal continues to twitch, as somewhere, its robotic guts are still at it, Mrs. Samuel notices, just before she is escorted roughly away. Yet she notes that the crowd is even more impressed by the insides of the robot. The people move forward despite the protests of several museum guards in blue uniforms. She sees them all point and gasp in turns at a metal rod, a leaking tube, a frazzled wire. They're asking themselves, *how did it work?* She doesn't understand the attraction, but it's there all the same. They gasp and want to get even closer to the impressive dinosaur, so real and so mechanical, nothing at all like Ollie's bare skeletons, she reasons as she is being driven away.

Piece for Piano Solo

For over a year she put up with Mr. Frohler's escapades, his loud bouts of drinking, when he would play on his upright piano for hours. "Improvisations," he called them, though most of them were indistinguishable from a small child pounding on the white keys and then the black keys, surprised each time by the difference in sound. These improvisations could last five hours at a time. Edna Stone would knock politely at the door at first, then louder, all to no avail. Occasionally, Mr. Frohler would answer her knock in his neat suit, tie still tight at the neck, a four-handed-Windsor. "Would you like a drink, madam?" he would say, his words distinct against a voice colored thickly with bourbon. She would shake her head no and beg him to at least play something recognizable on the piano, something the other tenants might recognize. He would accede and shut the door and soon out came a rendition of Tchaikovsky's Piano Concerto, or a similar bombast, which would ring out in the pre-war tiles of the hallways. Even Edna, who was admittedly tone deaf, had to admire his proficiency at the keyboard, at least when Mr. Frohler seemed to be trying. But then the droning of harsh chromatics and strange poundings would return, fixated and unbroken into the wee hours. Edna's solution was to turn up her old TV full blast on an unoccupied station so her small flat filled with the sound of white noise. Then she might, with luck, fall asleep. Edna wrote Mr. Frohler almost weekly about his conduct, but his lease was unbreakable, and it would have been cruel to do anything more. She had to learn to live with this old man above her. Besides, he was always polite and well-dressed. That was something, she told herself countless times, at least that was something.

Mr. Frohler would often sleep until noon, and Edna would sometimes be the one to wake him up, knocking gently on the door. She worried about the old man, who had no one, and who didn't seem to mind. "Everyone needs someone to watch out for," Edna told herself. Personally, she had her cats, one for each month of the year: short-haired ones she hadn't bothered to name, and the long-haired cold-blue Persians who preened themselves on the windowsill and only seemed to notice their environment when food was placed nearby. She didn't mind. Her cats asked very little of her, she asked very little in return.

Her husband Charles had died suddenly after a New Year's Eve party fifteen years ago. Edna had already been round and gray. She discovered that she didn't mind being alone. Charles never struck her or anything like that, but he did terrify her at times with that extreme temper of his. She still remembered the apoplectic look on his face as he collapsed into a mound at the foot of her bed that very last night. Charles carried his angry look into death, too. Even now, she felt guilty at times when she looked deeply enough and found she had perhaps wanted him gone. But then she had Charlotte, Augustus, and Ralph, her three regal Persians. They were all the family she needed. And, of course, her tenants, especially the ancient ones like Mr. Frohler. She didn't want the guilt of one day finding one of them dead and cold in their rooms without anyone noticing.

One Sunday night, as Edna knocked on Mr. Frohler's door, he cracked it a space and then opened it wide. "Please come in, madam. Please. Have just one drink with me."

Edna hesitated and thought for a moment whether Mr. Frohler was, at this particular point in time, dangerous. His eyes were no more reddened than usual. There was an old rank smell in the apartment, like old newspapers left in an attic, but no smell of alcohol. She would allow herself the pleasure of his company, if only to keep him away from his piano, which had been thundering on and off for the past two hours.

"Can I get you a drink?" he asked her.

She shook her head no. "I never touch any of that," she said.

"Coffee then?" he asked, motioning for her to sit on his ruined couch opposite a wooden crate used as an end table.

Edna nodded and straightened the folds of her black print dress as she sat down.

For a few minutes, Mr. Frohler was busy with his machinations in his kitchenette. Edna felt ashamed at how little space her tenants actually had. Their rent was not, after all, cheap.

Water in a large pan was soon boiling, and Mr. Frohler smiled from under his stooped shoulders as he poured the hot liquid over the instant coffee.

"Light or sweet?" he asked.

"Light and sweet, just a little," Edna replied. She was beginning to get a bit nervous in this cramped space. There was Mr. Frohler in his wrinkled gray suit and necktie with that large knot grabbing at his throat. He was a very proper gentleman, that was clear, she told herself. There was nothing on his mind other than neighborly conversation. He wasn't bad looking though, despite his rumpled dress. He still had a few wisps of gray hair left on his head. She noticed he stooped even more when he walked from here to there about the floor of the apartment. In his day, he'd been no doubt even more charming.

Mr. Frohler sat back down on a chair with a broken back opposite Edna. There was a less-than-comfortable pause. Then Mr. Frohler began to speak.

"I'll no longer be needing this apartment, you see."

"I'm sorry to hear that, Mr. Frohler." She wasn't really sorry at all.

"Call me James, please."

"Yes... James. You've found other lodgings, I suppose?"

"In a matter of speaking, yes," Mr. Frohler replied. "You see, I'm through with my work here."

"Your work? Yes, well, what precisely is that?" She imagined that he might be up to no good, running a confidence game out of his apartment, or perhaps something even more criminal.

"My music, for one thing. Then there is the matter of my autobi-ography."

Edna was beginning to chuckle.

"Your music? You mean you actually play the piano!"

"Oh yes. When I was younger I had commissions and everything." Now Mr. Frohler brightened. He told her that he had studied at the Peabody Conservatory of Music over sixty years ago. He had never gotten his degree, of course, but he was good enough as a trumpet and piano player to find work around the country in shows, playing in clubs, and for a few years, out in Hollywood. But when his teeth gave out, he no longer could play the trumpet. The piano was all that he had left. Edna was very thankful for this. She dreaded the prospect of hearing Reveille played at three A.M. in the morning.

"I wrote music for the cartoons."

"Cartoons?" Edna asked, now intrigued.

"Yes, cartoons. The old, good ones, you see. Every cartoon begins with a song. The pictures are drawn later to correspond to the music." Now he motioned modestly to himself with his thumb. "And I did the music."

"I see," Edna said, smiling. "I never imagined we had a real composer living among us."

She recalled going to the opera with Charles, a practice she had never done by herself since. She loved the drama, the costumes, the power of the music, though she was, she had to admit, quite tone deaf.

"Not to speak of my writings, you see," Mr. Frohler added.

"You're a writer of some sort, are you?" Edna asked.

"You might say so. When my eyes were good, I used to read every-thing. Never even thought of trying anything on my own. But when I got my operation for cataracts, I couldn't read anything anymore." He shook his head and then took off his glasses to show her how thick the lenses really were. "So, I started scribbling my thoughts down as well as I could, because it took much less time than reading. An hour here, an hour there. I used to have a nephew who came by and typed up all my jottings. Until he was killed in the Army, you see."

"I'm sorry to hear that, James," Edna replied. And she was sorry. She was growing comfortable with using Mr. Frohler's first name just as her coffee cooled sufficiently enough for her to drink it down in large gulps without blowing on its surface to first cool it.

"I've just completed my autobiography," he said. He had this odd shake to his head as he spoke, a tic that seemed only to show up when he talked, as if he were nervous about speaking in the company of other people.

Edna now planned to do something she couldn't have ever imagined herself doing before. She was going to ask Mr. Frohler to stay in her building. Instead of a blind drunk who pounded at his out-of-tune keys at all hours, here was a living and breathing artiste. It was so hard to hold an intelligent conversation with anyone else she knew. And perhaps Mr. Frohler would teach her to write herself. She was a voracious reader of detective stories and, occasionally, romances. Mysteries were her real interest, though. From the experiences of her own life, it was much easier to believe in a series of sudden and, at first, inexplicable deaths rather than an unbroken line of happy endings.

"I'm afraid that's not possible, you see," Mr. Frohler answered in response to her offer. He looked genuinely remorseful now; his eyes had lost their animation. It was truly sad the way his bushy eyebrows winced at the suggestion of staying in his apartment.

"If it's a question of rent, James..." Edna added. She was willing to haggle over rent—just a bit perhaps—in order to preserve her only artistically-minded tenant. Not too much, of course. She prided herself on being a keen businesswoman too.

"No, no. It's unalterable, I'm afraid." Mr. Frohler's eyebrows now raised themselves in a gesture of generosity, as if his large eyes behind his impossibly thick lenses could take in the whole world. "No, no. I like it here very much indeed," he said. "But I have other commitments."

"I'm very sorry to hear that," Mrs. Scheblenksy said. She offered to let him stay on as long as he'd like. She let him know, too, that she, anyway, had always appreciated his music. "The other tenants have always complained," she said, "But I have always told them that a talented man like Mr. Frohler needs to create whenever the urge strikes him. Isn't that right, James?"

"Thank you, Edna. There are very few people in the world as kind and as fair-minded as you," he said. Edna imagined that Mr. Frohler

winked at her. But perhaps it was just his tic affecting his right eye at a
suggestive moment. She thought now that he might change his mind
and stay after all. They obviously understood one another.

They finished several more cups of coffee and said good night like
old chums. Later that evening, Edna found herself actually enjoying
Mr. Frohler's piano shaking the innards of her building's rib cage. There
was a method to his mad tinkerings, apparently, if one only looked
close enough. She fell asleep anxious to tell everyone else she knew
about her artistic discovery.

Their meetings went on as before for about three weeks. Nearly
every night at about eight o'clock, Edna would politely knock and enter
Mr. Frohler's small apartment. She would drink coffee. He sometimes
sipped his bourbon instead. They talked about everything—family,
friends, politics, and most of all, Mr. Frohler's work. They talked about
poetry, jazz, old movies, the classics. He read to her in actual Greek
from Sophocles. One time they even watched a movie together on Mr.
Frohler's antique black-and-white set. That was their finest hour, she
thought. Also, Mr. Frohler had not been playing as much late at night.
This pleased her. When she was honest with herself, Edna found that
she still had no inkling as to what he could be up to with his piano.
From his discussions of the great works, from Bach to Rachmaninoff
to Charles Ives—impromptu lectures delivered from his own piano
bench complete with full-length excerpts from the great masters—
Edna was quite convinced that he was indeed some sort of real-life
musical genius. She sat and nodded approvingly at each move up and
down the keyboard, accomplished so skillfully by Mr. Frohler's thick-
knuckled fingers.

A month after their first meeting, Edna sensed something was
dangerously wrong. She knocked on Mr. Frohler's door at seven-thirty
one Thursday, coming early to see her new friend, anxious even, to
hear him play for her. But no one came to the door. She tried again at
eight, thinking that he was just out running an errand, and again there
was no reply. She called him on the phone from her apartment, but
again, nothing. She tried over and over that night and debated whether
she should open the apartment and check to see if he was okay, but
she thought that would be a violation of the terms of their friendship.

He was, after all, no ordinary tenant whom she could burst in upon whenever she liked.

She waited until Saturday morning at eleven to execute this particularly keen breach of trust, and when she opened the door, slowly and curiously, and dreading what she might find, she was surprised to find that the room was completely empty, save for the bare furnishings of the apartment. He had apparently moved out in the middle of the night a few days before. She stood there, shaking and puzzled, tapping her heavy-soled foot in the closed air of the apartment. She looked at his upright piano and imagined him sitting there, about to play for her, and felt like crying for a moment. Then she firmed up her resolve.

She would have to call her attorney, make sure the lease papers were in order, and then prepare the place to show it to someone else. Edna was surprised to see how automatic the whole process had become. She told herself that she couldn't afford to become attached to tenants, especially not those as old as Mr. Frohler, but this didn't seem completely convincing to her. She couldn't imagine why he didn't tell her he was leaving. If he told anyone in the building, he would have told her. She closed the door loudly behind her and proceeded to have lunch before getting to the business of cleaning up the newly emptied apartment. She fed her cats carefully, making sure that the three Persians got even more than their usual fair share.

She discovered the envelope while dusting away the remains of a life later in the day, inside the upper right-hand drawer of the battered roll-top which must have served as Mr. Frohler's writing desk.

She opened Mr. Frohler's letter carefully, not knowing what she'd discover. She didn't want a fuss for her other tenants, certainly no policeman should find this note, even if it indicated suicide. He deserved the respect of a funeral without suspicious mutterings. He deserved death by natural causes, if he were to turn up that way later, in the neighborhood or someplace else far from here. He deserved at least that. Her large brown eyes moved across Mr. Frohler's neat, cursive script, as she noticed that he did indeed write beautifully, a difficult task for someone supposedly so deep in the bottle and so visually impaired. Her wide cheeks huffed and puffed as she shifted the paper in her thick hands, and she adjusted her tortoise-shell spectacles to see better.

Sealed inside the envelope was a money order in the amount of several thousand dollars and a black-and-white photograph. The old and yet very distinct image showed a man in a thick mustache and a dark suit holding a baby with wisps of light hair on its head. The man was staring out with the cold gaze of those daguerreotype Civil War soldiers, eyes fixed on the newfangled camera before them, standing and sitting still for five minutes while their silhouettes took hold on silver, each one of them perhaps knowing that they would be dead the next day. This particular photo, however, looked like it was taken with a Brownie camera from an earlier time. It was a portrait of father and new son, presumably, but the infant looked out of place on his father's large knee. The man's stare itself might be fixed anywhere, thinking about his stock portfolio, on his game of squash at his club later in the day, on his ailing wife, who then was perhaps flat on her back with extreme sciatica in their suburban apartment, or on the bourbon after his match, its burning cool at the back of his throat. How much even then the man needed a drink. The resemblance to the real Mr. Frohler, at least as Edna remembered him, was immediately clear. If there were a person who had kept something of youth about him, even though age had wrecked his face and frame, it was Mr. Frohler. There was also a letter addressed to the child in the picture, where the money and letter should be sent. The apology was sincere and sentimental. *If I could only bring myself to send this*, he had written. Now it was up to Edna, or the police, or someone's attorney, to do this last deed. She was visibly tearing, and she wiped her left eye, smudging her makeup with a blunt finger.

She didn't know what to think about where the real Mr. Frohler could be. She imagined that he had been kidnapped, had been taken away by force, a victim of foul play, but this didn't mesh with the packed belongings. The apartment was stripped bare, carefully, with this one difficult exception. She thought of calling the police, maybe, to see if anyone had found a doddering and nearly blind man, one who could perhaps whistle quite well, wearing a gray suit, or worse, an unidentified corpse fitting this description. But then she got to cleaning up the place and decided that it was better to leave it alone after all. She would add her own letter, explaining things as best as she could, place a stamp on this one, and drop them both in the mailbox tomorrow as a token of their friendship. He deserved at least this consideration, if nothing else.

Lock

I went back to see what was left, to the apartment on Wind Road, to one building among many other identical buildings covered in beige aluminum siding and all built-up with cornices, landings, and windowsills that despite their intricacy were exactly, in every imaginable detail, the same.

Tiffany was supposed to be up in Baltimore visiting a cousin and recovering, I supposed, just like I was. It hadn't been an amicable parting. There had been more than words; the police had been summoned by a nervous neighbor and then warned away because we had worked it out between ourselves.

I parked my car and walked through the outer door, ducking my head under the low ceiling in the entranceway, the master architects of random symmetry were also inconsiderate of persons taller than six feet (when I relax and stretch out, I'm a good six foot four). The outer door was unlocked because this was still a polite Southern town. I passed through the hallway with its heavy carpet, which I happened to know had the identical texture of near-shag like every other hallway in this luxury condominium complex, except for local variations in color ranging from a royal red to a brown the hue of dirt. I climbed the stairs two at a time to the second floor, heading to Apartment L. I walked up to the door and unlocked it with my key without thinking. Tiffany had agreed not to change the lock, even though it was certainly a less than diplomatic sundering. She wasn't supposed to change anything. She hadn't changed the original lock, but none of my keys even remotely resembled the shape of one I imagined would fit into the new high-security lock mounted shoulder high—nearly waist-high for me, actually—above the knob on the door. I slammed an open palm into the wall reflexively but with too much force, because I hurt my hand. It didn't occur to me then that Tiff would have needed the extra security. Later, I flattered myself with the idea of her alone and nervous in the darkness, imagining all kinds of horrors in the shadows surrounding the parking lot in front of the building, or on the road beyond with its meager traffic, or in the wooded lot behind our apartment complex, with its gangly underbrush and Cyprus which seemed to reach out in that darkness after midnight.

I could only think of revenge as a motive for such new security. I walked over the narrow cement pathway that connected all of us in the complex, aiming for the super. I knocked on his door but there was no answer. I thought about leaving a note under the door but didn't have any paper. Then I went back to my car, lit a cigarette, and smoked it slowly, thinking on my days at this place. Though we had lived here almost two years, I never really got used to the layout of the buildings; I kept getting lost when visiting friends in the unalterable sameness of the complex. Now I had rented a renovated barn, a much more individual configuration, about forty-five minutes away and was, until this moment, quite happy with the way things had turned out. But I needed to check over some things at the old place. There were some clothes I knew I had left, and some books, and I admit I was curious at what it looked like now that Tiffany lived there alone.

I drove around town, making calls on my cell phone, searching the virtual yellow pages for a locksmith who could help me with my dilemma. I wanted someone discreet. Several times I dialed and hung up before there was an answer or before I could leave a message. Finally, I reached a human voice, almost by accident.

"I've locked myself out, out of my house," I told the voice on the other end of the line when it said hello.

"What's your name?"

"Donald Anthers," I told him.

"And where do you live?" the voice asked.

I gave him the address on Wind Road, the sound of which I always liked because it reminded me of names of places near water, streets in resort towns near windswept beaches, though we were hours away from any large body of water.

"I can give you directions," I said, fumbling a bit.

"Not necessary, my friend," the voice said, "I know where that's at."

I hoped that this guy wasn't the one who had installed Tiffany's new and vastly improved security system in the first place. I imagined this locksmith, whose first name was Blake, sitting around the phone hoping for some kind of misfortune like mine to disrupt the tedium of killing time around the shop. Nothing to do except listen to the radio, copy a few keys, and read *Locksmith Magazine* or something.

"There'll be a seventy-five-dollar road service charge, plus more if we break anything getting you in," Blake warned me.

That sounded high to me, but there was no time to waste.

"I need this done quickly," I said. "My wife isn't due home until tonight," I lied.

"Then maybe you don't need me," Blake suggested.

"Well, maybe not," I said, not believing any locksmith would throw away such easy money. "But I don't want to look the fool in this one; she'd never let me lose sight of it, not for a moment." I knew it would be too complicated to explain the real circumstances. In a strict legal sense, I had to admit, it wouldn't sound quite right, no matter how I managed to tell it.

"My friend, I know what that's like," he said. He didn't seem to mind that I might be lying. People like Blake must have heard all kinds of stories, people pretending to be someone else all the time in order to get into apartments, houses, parked cars. I imagined Blake to be someone who had to often sort out stories and wondered if mine sounded convincing enough.

Blake said that his woman friend was the same way, never let him sidestep his mistakes once he let himself slip.

"A barracuda, that one, her name's Lucille. A carnivore who eats prey—alive," he added.

"I know how that is myself," I replied, and remembered Tiffany at the very end. That last night she'd hurled a shoe at me, my own, size 13-1/2, a black dress shoe with a tall man's heel, careening in the dull light of the apartment. I'd watched it travel through the air, end-over-end. There'd been a kind of grace to its trajectory. But it didn't end very well for me. My ophthalmologist had said I had a detached retina in my left eye, only slightly detached. So, everything was slightly red for a week out of my left eye before I went in to see him. I also remembered that bright reddish white light he had used to heal me.

"I'll be there in thirty-five minutes," Blake promised.

I thanked him. That left me at least thirty minutes to get back to Tiffany's. I stopped at a drive-through and picked up two burgers and fries and large Cokes just in case Blake was hungry when he arrived, a gesture of good faith to the man who could save me.

***

"This one's not going to be easy," Blake muttered as he looked into the keyhole of Tiffany's brushed steel lock that guarded her door from intruders like me.

Blake in person was a man too young yet to be stout, but he would be, judging by the way he thanked me and stuffed his wide mouth with the burger I offered him and wolfed down the fries. As he moved to his knees to examine the lock and the frame, I noticed he shifted his weight sideways as if afraid to split his blue work pants.

He got back up on his feet, thought a bit, and opened his case. He pulled out a set of lockpicks, which weren't arranged in any particular kind of order. They were held together with a rubber band. He selected two wire-thin picks and turned toward me. "You sure you need this done?" he asked, looking up to me for approval.

I nodded.

"We'll try to tickle it first," he said, "before any heavy medicine," and he went right to work.

I pretended not to be too interested—I was fascinated—but I tried to stay out of the way. He turned his ear to the tiny instruments in his thick hand, which moved deftly, toward the lock, as if the solution would be whispered back to him. I noticed his fingers were remarkably even, like those of musicians I had known. I heard him swear, apologetically almost, just at the threshold of hearing. I thought it was important to be silent, to hear the click of the lock, like cracking a safe, perhaps, and wanted to ask if that was it, was it done by sound, but he seemed to have achieved such concentration that I just couldn't interrupt.

Just then someone came up the stairs. For a moment I thought I heard Tiffany's footsteps and imagined all kinds of legal complications. I would be arrested and booked for trespassing. I wondered if Blake here could pick handcuffs. Of course he could, I thought, as the steps rang out emptily in the stairwell, growing nearer until Blake looked up over his shoulder and then up at me for reassurance.

But it was a man wearing an attorney's light blue suit, whom I'd never seen in the building before. He looked up at us as he passed, I imagined suspiciously, with eyes of a trained legal mind about to begin cross-examination, eyes that looked larger than they should have, perhaps; he was wearing thick lenses with designer tortoise-shell frames. He opened as if he was about to speak, when Blake cut him short.

"Just helping Mr. Anthers get back into his apartment," he said, "It's all under control."

I noticed that Blake had skillfully palmed the two picklocks out of sight before the man could take notice.

I wasn't sure why the man took this to be true, except for the calm in Blake's voice. The man's oversized eyes narrowed a bit, and he tilted his head and looked at the lock next to Blake's shoulder.

"That's a piece of work," he said, motioning toward the lock, "I ought to get one myself."

"My wife's away on business," I ventured, "and I locked myself out." I watched his reaction to see if he perhaps knew Tiffany or that she had ended it with me, but he said goodbye and continued to walk up the stairs to the third and top floor.

"A shaker and mover," Blake said, and laughed at himself, returning to his work. He was much louder now. Apparently, his earlier delicate maneuverings weren't going to suffice. He held a kind of screwdriver in his right hand, wedged it between the doorframe, and jiggled the door with his left, his face now florid with effort. He was out of breath by the time he gave up. He wiped his hands on his knees, leaving sweaty marks on the denim there.

"Time for the heavy artillery," he said, "Have to go back to my truck."

He left his things in front of the door, and we walked out together into the cool afternoon air. I lit up a cigarette and offered one to Blake.

"Trying to quit," he replied, but he took one anyway.

He lit up almost surreptitiously and sent the match into oblivion with a snap of a heavy wrist. He drew deeply on his cigarette, exhaling with pleasure.

"Are you sure you want to do this?" he asked me off-handedly.

At first I didn't know what he meant. Then he pulled a two-handed drill from the cab of his green pickup truck, which I noticed had a bumper sticker that I read nervously. Police Athletic League.

"You said your girlfriend would be back this P.M.," he continued. "You should wait 'til then, and she could open it for you. Unless she forgot her key, too." He laughed to himself now.

I shook my head no and explained that she was flying back from Germany on business tonight or tomorrow, whenever she could get a connecting flight. "Business," I said, "you can't predict when these trips end."

Blake wasn't convinced.

"I couldn't get our super either," I said truthfully.

"It's your lock, I guess," Blake said.

"Sure it is," I said. I hope he believed me.

Back in front of the door, he assembled his portable drill.

"Carbide tips," he said, and the drill whirred suddenly in front of me, promising the dangers of thousands of revolutions per minute. "Just so you're sure," he said, lurching his whole frame around to the door. "We can punch a hole right here," he explained, pointing, "then we'll get better leverage on the bolt."

He smiled as he measured his work. With the drill off and placed in his left hand, he tapped the lock up and down its golden surface, listening with his left ear, feeling its stress points, for unsuspected flaws,

I imagined. I wondered if he had once been a real burglar, like you sometimes hear—people with a keen but antisocial talent for picking locks caught just once and then turning those same skills for the good of us all: old men and women and mothers and people like me who are locked out of their homes. I thought of how Tiffany would react to what was about to occur and instinctively massaged my left temple. I could have Blake replace the lock and give Tiffany and the super the new keys. But was it still breaking and entering?

I hesitated.

"Don't do it," I said suddenly.

He paused and let go of the trigger. He looked at me with a surprised and what I realized later was an almost malevolent grin.

"Is this really your house, Donald?" he asked.

I nodded. "It was," I said. "I lived here two years."

He stood there, the heavy piece of equipment straining the right side of his body.

"Look," he said, "I'm bonded, I can't do this, not unless it's your house." He twisted his neck around and fingered the hosel around his menacing bird's single black tooth. He searched in his pockets for something and pulled out the tool that he had used to tighten the bit. He loosened the drill's jaws, shook once or twice, and the blue-black bit fell out into his palm. He fingered its sleek steel spiral for a moment, confirming its sharpness. Then he made a motion to put everything away.

"You can't do this?" I said, incredulously. I didn't imagine someone like Blake could have any scruples. In his line of work, he must have heard constant excuses, stories made up to explain why someone and their property were now separate and that all identification, all means of knowing the truth were bound up inside the house, inside the car. Without the hard facts, it was up to Blake to decide.

"No" he said, "I can't." He paused and looked at me. "Not for the regular price."

"What do you mean?" I asked stupidly. I realized how foolish I must have appeared—a tall, clumsy fellow, kicked out of his lover's apartment and now wanting back in, wanting even more discomfort.

He looked me up and down.

"As far as I knew, until a minute ago, you live here," he said, pointing right at the lock, as if that in itself confirmed where I wanted to be. "Your girlfriend, your wife, whatever. That's no problem to me. I'm a professional. I look past the details." He fumbled in his pockets for his notepad, checking something. "That's sixty, seventy bucks," he said. "But now it's more complicated. If I break this lock, I'm an accessory to a crime, breaking and entering."

He positively chuckled with delight. He was enjoying my situation.

"Whatever it takes, I'll pay" I said without thinking. "You take credit cards—Visa? Mastercard? American Express?" I asked.

"Sure we do," he said. "And now we understand what we mean."

He moved swiftly and reached down to his bag, pulling out another attachment for the drill.

"Circle cutter," he said. "Tip of diamond. Synthetic." He brandished the drill with its new mouth, squeezed the handle, and the drill roared even more impressively. The diameter of its new bite, the circumference of damage, I took to be at least the width of my hand. The door stood no chance, I thought then. He would just carve a hole, reach in, and turn the bolt open with his own hand.

"Why don't we just kick it in," I asked.

He laughed. "Overkill," he said, and he made the first jarring contact, just left of the lock. There was a surprising amount of smoke and the heavy, sweet smell of paint and wood burning. Blake braced himself against the door, using two hands and all his weight against the torque of the machine. The door and its frame shook loudly, and I had the impulse to walk down the stairs and check how loud the noise was outside. But the hallway remained deserted. Anyone who heard us would never suspect a thief, anyway, I reassured myself, because the noise was so unbearably obvious. You'd have to assume we were doing some kind of necessary construction in the broadest daylight for everyone to see.

All at once, several layers of the door buckled from around the cutter and Blake swore as a spike of wood ripped loose and caught him on the hand, drawing blood, which splashed just one or two drops on the surface of the door. He dropped the drill with a loud thunk and wiped his hand on a green bandanna drawn from his back hip pocket.

I stared at him, not knowing what to do, really. He was a professional, I thought, and this mistake was somehow unthinkable, like a dentist slipping murderously with his drill or my eye surgeon careless with his red laser light, severing whole optic nerves, leading to a disastrous blindness. Sure, it happened more than you thought. But when it did go wrong, what could you do?

I stood there, offering to call someone, watching Blake bleed onto his handkerchief.

"Damned too theatrical," Blake said, and he wiped the wound, which was a nasty scrape on two or three fingers of his left hand. He said they wouldn't need stitches, but I wasn't so certain. Then he looked at the door intently, and I knew that he wouldn't give up then. He gathered himself up all at once—I'm a much taller man myself, but Blake seemed to acquire an even greater mass as he smacked the door with his right shoulder, the one not attached to his injured hand, and the wood and the door's metal hinges took the sudden shock.

But nothing else happened.

After a few minutes, he settled down, his hand-wrapped, and started working once more. Instead of the drill, which was retired carefully to its black nest, he chose a small, rather discreet looking hammer and a matching chisel to finish carving the circle begun on the door.

Half an hour later, we heard the sound of a thin circle of wood fall on the inside of the apartment. With his good hand, Blake reached in, found the lock, and turned it. Self-satisfied, he asked me to do the honors.

With the good key in the door, I turned the knob and pushed into the apartment. The door swung open onto a patch of afternoon sunlight, which slipped through the French windows onto the bare wooden floors. Only when we stepped into the light did I realize how dim it was in the hallway. We had been working without any direct light.

There were a few small cardboard boxes piled neatly on the far side of the room, a set of empty shelves, and a looming white couch that had come with the apartment, but little else in the place.

"Looks like someone got here first," Blake said to me now. He watched me for what I would say.

I stood there looking, thinking of my life before all this recrimination, lived within those four walls.

***

Weeks after that day, a letter came in the mail, postmarked from California, but I couldn't bring myself to read it until much later, after I could no longer resist. Tiffany had moved on, she wrote, and she was happy She enclosed a check for my half of the deposit on the apartment, which was a hundred dollars less because someone had broken the door down. "And in our old neighborhood," she had written. She felt much safer where she was now, and I had to agree.

Blake's bill came to two hundred and fifty dollars. I offered him three hundred, but he refused. As I paid him, he asked me, "What did you expect? What did she take that you were after?"

I looked out the window and didn't know what I should say. There were some clothes, some odds and ends, but I was sure that it must have been something else.

Mission

Ellie Lithgate closed her blinds before she sat down at her piano. She always did, and if you asked, she would say she valued her privacy. It wasn't that she was ashamed of her music, though it was true that no one else in town could have understood. People she knew were interested in livestock, football, their children, or going to dirt-track stock car races. Wednesday and Saturday nights spent at the Speed-O-Rama. And there she was, with her dogs and her music, playing in her white-framed house that sat on the edge of a small farm. The land behind her hadn't been plowed for years. Instead of corn or alfalfa, a haphazard grove of elms had sprouted up sometime around the turn of the century. When she bought the house two years ago after she and her husband separated for the last time, only the outline of the farm had been recognizable.

As she pulled down the shade now, she noticed the hulk of an ancient tractor, rusted away to a few ruined wheels and a dark mass of iron and weeds. She looked out on the back yard in the gray light of evening and narrowed her eyes, imagining she saw her raccoon, a twenty-pounder, which she had come to recognize. At least once a week, he rattled her garbage cans and frightened her two bloodhounds, Lavender and Methuselah, who often slept outside.

Every few nights, Ellie walked out onto her land carrying a bag of trash to burn. On colder nights, she warmed her hands over the strong-smelling fire. The raccoon, of course, was afraid of this light. But once, it had approached her from out of the darkness, its two eyes fire-bright and fixed in the outer limit of the flames. Flecks of ash swirled out and around the base of the fire, and the two of them had looked at each other, fascinated, each not knowing whether to be frightened or to move even closer. It was the raccoon who had backed away, succumbing to its natural instincts. Ellie had gone back to tending her fire. She felt somehow different after the experience. She suspected she was settling into her place by then, becoming a part of her environment. Even the animals around her tolerated her. But now as she closed the blinds, the shadow turned out to be nothing, a stray cat perhaps.

She turned toward her dimly lit music room, the largest room in the house, and began to play. One of the harpsichord suites by Telemann. The music filled the darkness of her small but comfortable home.

***

Ellie was a large woman, and proud of it, too. Broad-framed and long-limbed. She wore dark colors, black or dull sepia, and she was fond of hats. She needed no one here in the backwoods of the plains. She wanted nothing but her own time. She had saved enough money to live on while she was wintering, as she called it. Though she owned a pickup truck—an old blue Ford—she often just walked into the center of town for supplies.

One Saturday, she went into the A & P near the edge of the village. The bright aisles were filled by people in dungarees, farm children with flaxen hair from the strong sun, farm wives who were widening with the weight of maternal responsibility. Ellie kept to her shopping list strictly. She bought food for her dogs in cans, always the same brand, and lots of cereals, dry goods in bulk, and all sorts of fruits and vegetables for herself. The shopping cart she pushed was a cornucopia of light and color.

Her eyes searched the signs that marked each aisle for household goods. She needed to buy some bug spray for the ants in her kitchen. Every morning, she discovered a caravan of ants conveying her sugar and dried goods from her cabinets to a place underneath the refrigerator. This had to be stopped, and quickly, she'd decided.

As she turned her full shopping cart around the bend into the pesticide aisle, she was met with the cold glare of Marsha Gluckman, matron of the Gluckman Dairy Farm, who lived a mile or two up the road from Ellie and was herself pricing cans of roach spray. Her two plump children Benny and DeeDee were hanging on to her cart, rocking it back and forth. Benny was teasing his sister, who was a year or two younger and taller than he was.

"Good morning, Marsha," Ellie offered. They had met at Sunday service a few times and knew only the barest circumstances of each other's lives.

"Morning," Marsha replied. There was a strong, almost Appalachian, twang to her voice. She was a thin woman who prided herself on getting things accomplished. She ran half her husband's dairy business, and the word about town was that he was a bit of a drunk and that without her they might well have gone under.

"Haven't seen you at service lately," Marsha asked, "Hope you haven't been sick or anything."

Ellie knew what Marsha was really thinking. The children had stopped tearing at each other's hair and were staring at the large woman dressed in a dull brown dress and black overcoat. Her hat was draped over the edge of the metal cart. Their large eyes showed a remarkable fear, what might have been reserved for a freak at a freak show or someone who had lost an arm in an accident. Though they had surely been told otherwise, they couldn't help but stare.

Ellie could only speculate. *What have you told them about me*, she thought to herself. *Am I some sort of witch? Is that it?*

"No, nothing like that. I've been attending the First Church lately," Ellie said. The truth was she had stopped going entirely. She was tired of the whispers and strange glances she got from the regulars at the services. She was the outsider, a divorced woman, presumably wealthy (though this was not so), who couldn't be placed within their tiny structure of the town. She could only create problems, start affairs, break up homes, perform vicious rites of animal sacrifice, and whatever odd visions these peoples' simple mores managed to conjure.

"Sorry to hear that," Marsha said. Her voice twanged self-righteously, undisguised. *We don't need you around*, she was really saying. But Ellie didn't care, which apparently bothered Marsha to no end. Like everyone else in the town, Ellie knew Martha disliked what she couldn't comfortably place. That's the way the town has gotten along for so long, Ellie thought to herself. Only by distrusting the world outside can it protect itself.

They parted company politely, the children coming back to life once they passed out of range of Ellie's odd spell. Marsha guided her cart accurately away from her, and Ellie chose her supplies more quickly now, anxious to get back to feed her dogs, to the comfort of her music and the quiet of her house.

***

At one time, accusing voices, like misdirected prayers, often whispered their presence to Ellie, but they now spoke with less and less regularity after the divorce. She assumed it was because she had somehow failed to live up to the vocation demanded by her husband, the Reverend Butler Zachariah Yates. It was true, Reverend Yates had once more gone to the Far East, this time to the Ivory Coast, and she had refused, without even thinking about the possibility of packing up her things and moving to yet another continent. She had just known. The answer had come from the part of her that was unsuspected and undoubtedly real.

"Big work to be done there," the Reverend had proclaimed. "The ministry is building a new church, a new school, and a medical clinic."

He hadn't even bothered to ask whether Ellie would be interested in going abroad. He was a cathedral of a man: tall, statuesque, buttressed by arms that gestured theatrically as he sermonized to his congregation. Even when alone with Ellie, he was prone to these kinds of gestures, and they had long stopped talking as two equals. She could only ignore these private sermons and then respond with what she really thought of him.

Years earlier, Ellie had lived in Malaysia with the Reverend, where his grand plans had failed to materialize. The money had simply run out. More likely (she could never be certain—the Reverend was continually evasive when it came to his finances), the money had never existed. She had shared three years of backbreaking labor with her husband. They had left behind a few thankful people and the cement foundation of a small hospital, which was abandoned at the edge of the jungle to be filled up by tropical rains.

Maybe the Reverend would try this again, but Ellie was not so gullible. She had demanded the separation, not him. At that precise moment, she knew he could see she had not lived up to the calling, presuming he thought that she had failed him. He didn't even try to convince her otherwise.

"You have to be comfortable with your own soul," he had told her.

And she was, entirely, she thought then.

Ellie had moved out the next day to her sisters in Chicago.

The divorce was finalized a year later, give or take a few days. She had received a letter and a photograph of the Reverend Yates shaking hands with another smiling man in a suit, the two of them cutting a gigantic yellow ribbon in front of a stretch of grasslands near the city of Abidjan in the Ivory Coast. Both men were smiling as though the groundbreaking in itself had been an impossible feat. He wished her well. He blessed her. And she thanked him for it.

Afterward, in her dreams, she seldom saw the angry face of Reverend Yates anymore, and she heard a truer, inner voice telling her that she was all right, after all.

After she had moved to her new place, she found she could sleep right through to the morning without being tormented anymore by the night's demons. Usually, she awoke to her dogs barking. After she fed them, her own breakfast was the best meal of the day—bacon and cereal and thick, buttered, slices of toast. She would read the *Kansas City Star*, which came by mail the previous day, and sit with her feet on a chair in her kitchen, thinking and eating and maybe humming a little to herself.

There was no need to think about what she could be missing in the tropics, though at odd moments the figure of the Reverend came back to mind, a figure who rattled the leaves of the jungle of thought before he pounced into view. But she was quite happy right where she was.

***

The local Gophers were a truly average football team, but in their mediocrity they somehow inspired almost religious devotion from their fans. After a particularly closely fought loss to the Louden City Homesteaders, their archrivals from across the state, a group of drunken teenagers from the high school, which was also unremarkable except for the mediocrity of its faculty and students, managed to vent their anger on the unsuspecting Ellie. She awoke from a fitful sleep to find that her yard was torn up by deep grooves of a four-wheel-drive pickup truck. Methuselah had been shot with what must have been a pellet gun, according to Dr. Larcher, the local vet, who bandaged the animal while Ellie looked on and patiently listened. Throughout the whole procedure, she kept her composure.

"Happens every year," he said, shaking his bald head like he had seen too much of the same thing for too long a time.

She just nodded and petted Methuselah's one good ear. The other one had been torn badly and required several stitches.

"Thank you for your help," she told the doctor as she left.

He had been very kind, but Ellie found herself disliking him, since he, as much as anyone, was part of the fabric of the town. He had treated the pets and farm animals of the town for over three decades.

She drove too fast on the way home in her truck, both dogs riding shotgun with her in the cab. When she got home, she cried as she made a bed for them inside the house. She called the sheriff's department to find out if there were any more leads, but there was nothing. Several of her neighbors had called the night before to report a noisy group of teenagers, but none of them had any of their pets attacked so viciously. The sheriff's deputy said he was sorry he couldn't do any more for her.

Because she was so full of sadness, Ellie lit candles throughout the house and found herself muttering under her breath to her ex-husband. She was sure that she didn't deserve to be punished like this, but part of her kept nagging that she did and she promised herself out loud that she would never let anything like this happen again.

That night, there was a low moon over the old cornfield; it grew to an impossible size in the darkness over the clumpy shadows of the trees. In the dirty orange flames, Ellie burned her trash and told the wind that whoever did this didn't know how much pain they had given her and that all she wanted was to keep to herself. She thought she saw eyes peeking out of the semi-darkness cut out by the moon but wasn't sure. She even saw a few bats careen into the distance; their high-pitched screams thrilled her. In that moment, under the quiet sky, she decided never to be afraid again.

She hummed to herself and played her harpsichord that night while the dogs howled themselves to sleep, the three of them singing in the music room in the candlelight. Her tears had stopped themselves as she played some of her favorite Scarlatti. As the music began to toy with itself and echo in polyphony, her tears, at least one or two of them, returned, and then she found she was truly happy, at least for the moment.

***

Ellie put on her robe of pink cotton to answer the knock at the door. She expected someone with car trouble, perhaps, or worse, someone who had an accident on the dark flat roads that invited people to travel too fast for their own good.

She knew before she opened the door who it was. She saw the hulking outline of the black Lincoln Continental in the waning moonlight. Despite his finances, the Reverend always managed somehow to drive with style.

"Ellie!" he said, reaching out for her. He was larger-than-life, larger than she remembered him, anyway. She met his embrace with fear and a measured anticipation.

"Zachariah," she said, her heart and lungs threatening to give out from the force of emotion. "What in God's name brings you here?"

She invited him in, of course, and he acted as if he were genuinely grateful. He said he was traveling through the Midwest on a speaking tour to raise money for the Ivory Coast mission. Ellie had been right, the money had run out. The Reverend had contracted a particularly virulent type of dengue fever, and he had to come back to the States to convalesce. Now he was getting his momentum back, and finances, to continue the work of the Lord.

"Those people need us," he said, putting his coffee down to illustrate the seriousness of his mission with large gestures of his hands. "I've seen babies who were too sick to cry, children who go blind as soon as they're old enough to walk and find water contaminated by parasites."

"That's all right, Zachariah," she interrupted. "I've heard you describe all this before." I lived it, too, for six years, right along with you, she reminded herself.

The Reverend paused and considered his situation.

"I just need to hole up a few days here til Sunday. I'm to speak at your church and a few others up and down the Interstate."

Then he looked at the white trim of her robe, up and down, like he was considering something else. Her eyes must have registered a frozen lake upon which the Reverend wouldn't dare tread. There were weak points on this ice where he could fall right through, down into the cold, deep waters of her heart. But the Reverend liked danger, he liked this business of exploration. It was in his missionary blood.

"Then I have some time of my own."

He shifted on the blue fabric of the couch, rubbed the side of his sunburned face, and moved his jaw back and forth like he was testing whether his teeth were in the place he expected them to be. He looked up at her expectantly.

"We'll have to see," Ellie said.

She offered to sleep on the couch while he could sleep upstairs in her bed, an offer she knew he would refuse due of his code of a Southern gentlemen that she had always found ridiculous.

There was a particularly uncomfortable moment when he gave her a polite kiss on the cheek. It resurrected old memories in her, some terrifying, some beautiful.

She wished him goodnight and walked slowly upstairs, uncertain of what the Reverend could be up to this time.

***

Both services turned out to be packed, a result of the end of harvest season, which had been successful though unremarkable after a June drought that had threatened everything. The people were thankful and tired. They came to the brick and glass church out of comfortable habit, to sit among themselves and think about the past few months. Some were even planning vacations, or what equipment they needed to pay to fix or to buy. Some were just worried about making the payments on their land, their home, their tractors, or their cars. None of them were particularly wealthy, but this was the one time of year they could consider buying something extra, even indulgent, for themselves, for their spouses, for their children. In the middle of the congregation, Ellie sat on the bare wooden pew, anxiously waiting for the Reverend to speak for the second time. She had already seen the generosity of these people at the eight o'clock service; the wicker collection basket was overflowing with green. She wondered whether the ten o'clock crowd would be any different. In this batch of worshippers, she recognized more people: the Terrences, one of the oldest and largest landholders in the county; the Gluckmans, Marsha and Jake and their kids; and the Horaces, who owned a lumberyard. This was certainly the right crowd for Reverend's missionary magic, she thought.

The second time through his routine, the Reverend Yates was even more perfect. From the instant the regular preacher—a shortish but spry, white-haired man, Reverend Camden—introduced him, the Reverend Yates was in extremely fine form. Ellie was reminded how gifted a performer he was from the very start, the way he disguised his height and his bulk at the beginning of his talk. He almost shuffled up to the microphone, burdened by the weight of missionary responsibility. At certain moments, he would unveil the length of his arms, as though in soliloquy with himself. "What then must we do? Tolstoy—remember, a religious man—once asked himself." The answer, the Reverend Yates suggested, was to rescue the children. And then he looked out onto the small ones in the audience, pointing with two of his large fingers. Ellie noticed that some of the mothers, especially those that carried their children in their arms, found themselves crying. The men, of course, did not. But they stroked their beards and pondered their own luck, especially this year with the July rains that had saved everything. They contrasted this with the Reverend's land, where nothing grew. Though Ellie knew the Reverend Yates failed to mention that in the Ivory Coast, the problem was carving out land to farm from the tremendous growth of the rainforest. He had discovered a long time ago that people appreciated the problem of poverty when it was described in terms of deserts, not the overbearing fecundity of the tropics.

Then Ellie had a moment of tremendous and unforeseeable embarrassment.

From underneath the hot lights and height of the podium, the Reverend motioned downward with his great hands and mentioned that the reason he was able to carry on his work in the deserts and jungles of faraway lands was the tremendous devotion of his former wife Ellie, who was sitting and living amongst them at this very moment.

Ellie shifted her weight at this. (It was true, she had drifted off into a near-sleep, thinking about planting a garden herself next year. It would be nice to grow something out of the earth, too.)

Now, suddenly, she was an object of great curiosity. The crowd murmured to itself at who was the lucky party in their midst doing such fine work. Finally, with growing applause, the Reverend demanded that Ellie stand up, which was difficult since she found herself so dizzy that she wanted to pass out. But she stood, reluctantly and a bit unsteady, careful to flatten out as inconspicuously as possible the folds in her brown dress which were ironed into the fabric from sitting still for so long.

The crowd had an odd reaction, which was not lost on Ellie. At first the clapping seemed to pause, like a moment of stillness before a thunderstorm. Ellie caught the surprised look of Marsha Gluckman,

Cheryl Terrence, and others who had never tried to understand her. But now, in parallel acts of charity, they forgave themselves of their initial suspicions of Ellie, and then broke into a louder, stupendous, and sustained clapping. The Reverend thanked them for their charity from the podium. Ellie wobbled and bowed her gratitude from her pew.

At the very end of his talk, almost as an afterthought, the Reverend reminded his audience that the proceeds from the first pass of the collection basket would go to his Ivory Coast mission. As the collection basket came round, Ellie found herself prying open her purse and searching for her wallet before she realized what she was doing. Instead, she found a tissue and used it to wipe the corners of her eyes and nose. She wasn't used to receiving this kind of attention. After the service, she waited in her pick-up truck for the Reverend, who had left his car parked in her driveway far from the road. As Ellie sat in the cab of her truck and people streamed by on the way to their cars, greeting and chatting with each other, they waved to her, laughing and smiling. Ellie found herself smiling and waving back. She wondered what was keeping the Reverend, but she didn't mind waiting, though these people made her uncomfortable still.

***

There never was any question of the two of them reconciling themselves to each other, not on their old terms, but they went through the motions anyway, to assure themselves that they had tried everything. The Reverend was due in Kansas City that very evening.

"Thank you for putting me up," he said. "I hope I wasn't too much trouble."

The Reverend's wide cheeks were still flushed from the excitement of the morning and the hour or two he and Sarah had spent inside the house, in her kitchen, talking and reassuring one another.

"It was no trouble, Zach," she said. "It was nice seeing you again. It really was."

Now she felt strangely sad, like this might be the last she saw of him.

"When are you going back, Zachary? When is that?"

"Oh," he said, "not for a good long while."

The Reverend toyed with the satchel which stood next to his side on her porch.

"I've got quite a bit of speaking to do," the Reverend said. "I want you to have it," he suddenly said, motioning to the heavy bag. It was filled with the proceeds from several months of the Reverend's sermons.

At first, Ellie was shocked. "No, I couldn't," she said, "What about the mission?"

"There is no more mission," he said. "There was a suspicious fire. And the government took back my visa." He wasn't going back, not to the Ivory Coast, anyway. Besides, he had gotten sick. It took him longer to get his strength and energy back now that he was getting to be an old man.

Trying not to think about it, she decided to take the money, knowing that she might not see him again and that he might be lying anyway about where the money would go if it stayed in his hands. This gift was his way of marking his last exit.

They embraced and promised to write one other, though she didn't even have his address. Ellie heard the crunch of the gravel as his black Continental edged down her driveway. He waited a moment for a semi-truck to go down the road, and for a spilt second she had a terrible and strangely satisfying image of him backing out into the truck's path, his car transformed into a twisted, smoking hulk of metal with him emerging unscathed, miraculously, from the tomb of the wreckage. But he waited patiently for the truck to pass and paused while he shifted into gear. Through the dark tint of glass, she saw him give her a salute with the two fingers of his right hand. She responded with the smallest of gestures, an open palm held at shoulder height for only a second. She turned as he tooted his horn and went back to her house to feed the dogs, who always howled uncomfortably when there was company in her driveway.

Everybody needed calming down.

***

That night was moonless, and as Ellie walked down her path to the trash barrel, she knew she was being watched. Her orchard was alive tonight. She could imagine the giant eyes of owls, the eyes of her raccoon who had lately figured out that he could chew through the rope Ellie used to tie down the garbage cans and eat his fill. So, she had to make sure that she burned her trash more regularly.

The fire lit easily, but as she added the refuse of her days with the Reverend into the flames, it burned more slowly. Then it caught firmly and actually managed some heat in the chill autumn air. Her hands stung her as she held them in front of the flames. There was enough money for her to get something she had always wanted. She had placed a few calls to a company in Boston. The grand piano would be shipped by truck over the next two weeks. There was plenty of space in her music room for an addition to the family. She felt herself surrounded in the warm tones of her music, which was, after all, not her own but something that was older and more profound than anything she had experienced. There was solace in this, and in the darkness that surrounded her now. Ellie let herself be hypnotized by the flames and only walked back to her home when she was good and sure that everything had been burned up. She turned her back to the orange ashes and starless sky and walked toward her house, now humming, now whistling to herself, anxious to get back inside.

Frontier

That night, Cosmo met Moscow in a diner named Mahmoun's. Cosmo walked up to his friend in short, hesitant steps. Before he sat down, and before he noticed Melissa sitting cross-legged in the seat across from Moscow, her long legs and feet folded mysteriously underneath on the sticky red vinyl of the diner booth, Cosmo first heard his voice. Moscow was talking, with his usual excitement, about the demise of the old West.

"Imagine what the Sioux thought," Moscow was saying, "when the first locomotive rolled across an open plain clotted with buffalo—miles of hide, bristle, horns, and hooves!" Moscow's voice grew uncomfortably loud as he looked over to Cosmo, who had taken off his baseball cap. He motioned for Cosmo to sit down, luckily, he thought, next to Melissa. At first, she didn't acknowledge him, but then she nodded and managed an uncomfortable smile. Like two schoolchildren, they had talked surreptitiously on the phone several days earlier. They agreed that they would tell Moscow of what had started between them. The problem was… betrayal wasn't something you came out and just announced, and Cosmo had thought hard about how to broach the subject. But right now, Moscow was in his own world, unstoppable in his own way.

"The hunters just stuck their rifles out of their Pullman cars. They used the window frames for balance, to take aim. It was like shooting ducks. Pointless, craven slaughter!" Moscow cackled with a manic historian's delight. He motioned with his long hands across the room, suggesting a suitable vista. "They slaughtered thousands in a single afternoon," he went on. "More than a whole tribe could take in a decade!" Moscow now pointed across the table at Cosmo, right between his eyes. He pulled an imaginary trigger. Melissa looked at him too. Cosmo knew she probably imagined the hulking bodies in the bloodied dust as well. She was a bit prone to visions herself, and so the two of them, Moscow and Melissa, were certainly dangerous together. At times, Cosmo almost disliked being around them. But there was that other thing, the way Melissa inhabited the territory of his dreams. She was like gravity, an unseen and undeniable force that couldn't be dismissed. Certainly in the way she ordered his universe lately.

Moscow was wild with his story by now.

"They thought it was the end, that the entire culture would be obliterated!" Moscow gesticulated, knocking his coffee over. Melissa, without missing a syllable, grabbed a wad of white paper napkins and began mopping it up. Cosmo saw the pool of coffee, a steaming continent, threaten the edge of the table and Melissa's lap. But she escaped. She looked intently over her wire-rimmed glasses onto the table as if enchanted by the fine droplets that trailed after her hand as she wiped the table. Cosmo noticed the silver bracelet around her wrist, no doubt a gift from Moscow. She looked frail somehow, almost intellectual, but he knew she was deceptively strong from her days as a long-distance runner.

Moscow thanked Melissa and then moved forward in his seat and continued.

"They knew it when they saw the line of smoke and heard the reports, almost imperceptible in the distance. They knew in an instant where it was all headed, toward extinction." Moscow moved his hands emphatically. "They might have told themselves later that it was impossible, that their way of life had endured so long, how could it go the way of the buffalo? But I think, deep down, they knew. The Wild West was one atrocity after another!" Moscow brushed his hair back on his head and smiled, quite exuberantly. He was clearly pleased with his performance.

Melissa nodded and agreed with his strange pronouncement. No one had been drinking yet, not even Cosmo, and it was usually difficult to take Moscow straight up, Cosmo thought; he needed a chaser. He needed to be pulled back gently from Moscow's fantasies. Otherwise, he might think Moscow was only a lunatic, but he was much more than that; a self-educated carpenter, a gourmet cook, there were even rumors that he had done time years ago for some kind of white-collar crime. Moscow didn't like to reminisce about himself, though. He would much rather talk about his latest discoveries.

Moscow then launched into a speech about why Italian Renaissance painters were better than anyone else. He had been to Italy on a vacation. Instead of snapshots or slides from his trip, Moscow came back with his nearly empty suitcases and a mind filled with new theories about everything, from wines to Europe's high-speed rails. Cosmo honestly wished he had brought the snapshots instead. Moscow said they took Italian boys at six and forced them to paint until they were grown men. They studied under the hands of a master for two decades before they were turned loose to do any of their own work.

"I think that's the best way of doing it," Moscow said. "But what do I know? What do any of us know?"

"You do pretty well," Melissa said.

Cosmo watched Moscow, still self-satisfied, touch Melissa's hand. Without making a show of it, she withdrew hers and held it under the table on her lap.

Cosmo now coughed to announce himself officially. He, anyway, felt like he was there in the room, even if no one else took notice.

"Hello, Cosmo," Melissa said, finally.

"Good to see you again," Cosmo offered. When Melissa turned her head to him, he shuddered. He was dizzy with near infatuation. On the mirror that lined the booth behind them, he noticed that his short black hair was a mess.

"No wonder nobody ever says hello to me," Cosmo said. "I look depraved."

"Depravity is only a state of mind," Moscow said.

They all nodded at this. They had seen each other in their most frazzled states; it was perhaps a definition that all understood.

Melissa had always wanted to be Moscow's disciple, Cosmo had thought, but now he wasn't so sure. Usually, he could tell from the way her eyes took in Moscow's every word, the way the corners of her lips opened with just a hint of wonder. But lately she didn't seem to be interested. She was wearing a T-shirt, shocking white, against her authentic summer tan.

"The Italian painters…" Moscow went on. Cosmo stifled a groan. Melissa shifted uncomfortably in her seat.

After he was through, and even Melissa looked a little worn, Moscow looked discreetly at his watch, a silver contrivance with inner dials that indicated the time in all the major time zones across the world. He looked once quickly left and then right. Then he looked serious.

"I gotta get out of here!" He put both hands on his head, feigning a migraine. "Melissa! Quick! Where's the car!"

Apparently, Melissa didn't get his joke. She unknitted her eyebrows and put on a hurt look. Cosmo thought it was disgusting, the way he manipulated her. She was very nearly in his quiet clutches, and she didn't even know how close she was from his perversity. It was almost touching, her potential to be rescued.

"Why, on the side of the building where we parked it," she said.

Moscow positively howled, "Well, for God's sake, Melissa, go get it!"

And she looked back at him blankly.

"I'm sure it's all right," she said. "Cooper's on guard. He'll protect it."

"Cooper," Cosmo winced, "is only one dog, and there are many thieves."

"By definition," Moscow nodded. Cooper was, after all, a Shar-pei, a ridiculous creature, or so Cosmo thought, and rather desperately sad in a way. Over time, the dog's sagging Shar-pei skin had folded further and further away from its frame. Cooper was also almost toothless by now—a product of veterinary dentistry—and old age had taken away most of a bark that the dog never really possessed anyway.

After paying the check, the three of them walked out of Mahmoun's. Moscow left three coffee-stained dollars under a tall glass of ice.

***

Around the side of the restaurant in the failing July sun, the dog was asleep in back seat of Melissa's '79 Gran Torino Convertible, a reclining buddha of sorts with his muzzle wedged between the middle of the beige vinyl, simulated-rawhide seats. Cosmo sat uncomfortably next to the unmovable dog who won't budge, even with a not-so-subtle push into dog's ample middle.

"Some watch dog," Cosmo remarked.

Melissa took the wheel and Moscow rode shotgun.

"To the wars!" Moscow shouted while adjusting his side view mirror. He liked to comment on the action in front of and behind him. Cosmo adjusted his baseball cap and pretended to snooze, too, though it wasn't possible, not with Melissa driving. She was a miraculous driver, with a stock car racer's gift for speed, downshifting around turns, and sudden and facile acceleration. Cosmo was compelled to watch her skill at the wheel.

They were going to Club Antaeus, where Moscow's friend's band was playing. They pulled out onto the expressway, and Melissa moved surefootedly into traffic. She was wearing black gloves despite the humidity and Armani prescription shaded glasses against the light of sunset. Her hair flowed behind her magnificently, Cosmo thought, and he caught himself smelling the air behind her, drafting her, he supposed, hoping to catch something of her scent. But the air was curiously neutral. Cosmo could smell nothing except the open highway on a summer night.

Melissa weaved lithely between semi-trucks loaded with heavy cargo— pig iron, tubing, livestock, and mini-vans. She accelerated magically past middle-aged folks with stern stares and cars made in Scandinavia that were designed against all kinds of impact and angles with belts, bags, and restraints and whose drivers still seemed intently worried about the mauve blur of the convertible as it blitzed past. And Melissa never did flinch as she added up her victims, the people she passed.

Over the thirty-five miles to their destination, Moscow became fixated on comets. "Comets," he said, "have always been taken for signs, even by the most advanced cultures," he said. Cosmo nodded, of course, but was mostly interested in the curve of Melissa's neck as she floored it past some local in a sea-blue Mercedes.

"Take Comet Kahoutek," Cosmos heard Moscow say quizzically, "It comes back once every 75,000 years, but how do we know if it really makes it?"

Cosmo now imagined they were inside a comet, an object made of heated metal and speed. Melissa was driving them round the Milky Way. Looking at her shades in the rear-view mirror, Cosmo was titillated with the possibility that she too was watching him carefully (she didn't seem to need to watch the road. *Would he?* Cosmos asked himself. Not if it were such a natural alignment of forces to be moving so effortlessly).

Moscow was oblivious to his surroundings, and Cosmo considered taking a few chances. He could slide his hands around Melissa's shoulders and rub her neck and back to help her relax while driving. But that would, he suspected, cause her inertia to be violently disturbed. Melissa would likely wrench them into a ditch (the monster convertible, unlike the Volvo, didn't even have seatbelts. Melissa said they had been removed by the previous owner in a sort of fit of confidence over the car's immense physical dimensions that gave one a feeling of distinct invincibility). But if they did leave the road, Cosmo thought they would go tumbling, head over heels, as they were thrown from the open car. Or, he imagined, he might be pinned in wreckage next to Melissa, the both of them unhurt. Perhaps he would have a slight bruise that would look purple and discolored as much as possible without causing pain (because he hated the thought of pain). Melissa could wait with him until help arrived, while Moscow could be thrown clear of the wreckage entirely but perhaps knocked out and not there to bother them.

Cosmo petted the sleeping Cooper instead, who didn't even stir from slumber. It was too hot for anything but sleep for the dog. Cosmo realized the danger of moving too close to Melissa at this moment. He kept thinking that she was eyeing him in time with the traffic, with the radio. *Was there a hint of a smile on her lips?* Cosmo now thought to himself. It was difficult to distinguish Melissa flirting with him from a gesture of satisfaction at having passed a Winnebago loaded with hunters, a large vehicle wearing Kentucky plates.

Cosmo thought that he knew the value of waiting.

"Some comets go round the edge of the solar system," Moscow expounded. He had turned his head toward Cosmo, and even Cooper reared his head to look at this disturbance and even managed a hint of a muted growl. The dog dropped his head down to the vinyl as Moscow waved his heavy arm out straight, like a cane in the air, just above Melissa's head, to illustrate an astronomical point-of-fact.

"Some comets do come back," Moscow repeated. "They're at war with the velocity stolen from the objects they escape from. They're sling-shotted. If they miss the earth or another planet, they're given an extra pull as a reward. But this pull may not let them make the turn back, to give them another run in a couple thousand years."

Moscow nearly poked Melissa's right temple. She looked over to him and let off the accelerator. Cosmo thought her spell had been shattered by Moscow, but she was turning off the ramp toward Club Antaeus, their new center of gravity for the evening.

Melissa didn't seem interested in Moscow's stare. It was a look of longing, Cosmo thought then, of one body used to the orbit of another around a point of fixed distance between them, an imaginary coordinate that had, perhaps, shifted away from Moscow and was now drifting further and further away.

"At what point does the comet give way?" Cosmo asked. "When does it decide not to come back? At what exact distance?" he asked Moscow, who had to think awhile before beginning his answer.

***

Club Antaeus began underground. Its doors were sunken into the pavement. Already there was a crowd in queue. Moscow led Melissa by the hand down into the earth, from Cosmo's perspective, anyway. It was a club with dark wooden tables and cement walls that provided the same acoustics as a parking garage. The band, which was called Milk of Wonder, was doing a sound check, fiddling with cables, Marshall amps, and effects racks that flashed star-like in the still dim stage like exotic stereo equipment. Meanwhile, Moscow talked about why he wasn't up on stage, too, with his friend Max, the percussionist.

"Not a drummer," Moscow said, "We're percussionists." He tapped rhythmically with the beer glass in front of him, as if to illustrate his nervous percussive energy. "I would have been a musician," he continued, "but when I discovered, ten years after the fact, mind you, Johnny Rotten of Sex Pistols and his massively classic recording of God Save the Queen, I was floored. Almost totally." Moscow now crossed himself. "I had seen God, and he was weeping, too." He cleared an imaginary tear with a finger. "Here I was, trying to be a percussionist with my drums and my expensive synthesizers and electronics, and somebody gave these criminals second-hand instruments, and they came up with this music that I was trying so hard to invent myself."

Moscow looked over to the stage. The stage lights had suddenly gone up on the band, which was on the precipice of starting its first set.

"That's when I finally gave up," Moscow said. There was something lost in his expression now, contemplating the outline of his empty bottle.

Cosmo looked to Melissa, who was unconsciously peeling the label away from a bottle that couldn't be hers. She was drinking wine.

"I need another drink," Moscow said, "Do you want one?"

He left into the darkness, silently, just as the room exploded into sound. The band was pounding into its first song.

"Dramatic exit," Cosmo said to Melissa, who couldn't possibly have heard him. He gazed at her in the earsplitting dimness. She was looking back at him. Her lips moved soundlessly; they were fluttering. Cosmo speculated on when Moscow would come back, when would his trajectory take him round this part of the room again? The bar was crowded, milling with people. Cosmo picked up Melissa's left hand in his own. It was weightless, until she kissed him. She made the first contact, though he leaned off his stool into her path. They kissed for only a few seconds. They couldn't talk because of the bombast around them, and Cosmo was thankful. They would talk later. They had shifted their chairs toward one another. A new alignment, one that set subtle forces in motion between them, would grow with a sudden magnitude. They would fall toward each other from opposite directions. Once set in motion, it was perhaps irrevocable. At least Cosmo hoped so.

He felt a hand tapping his shoulder. Melissa's eyes told him it was Moscow, who handed him another beer and seemed to mouth the words that it was on him, or something similar. Cosmo couldn't be sure that Moscow had noticed anything. Despite all his knowledge, Moscow was still unaware of most of what went on around him.

Milk of Wonder finished its first set with a particularly high-decibel song that Cosmo really liked but it left his ears, and he suspected everyone else's, blown and ringing. So, it took him a few seconds to realize what Moscow was saying.

"I got to get out of here," Moscow said. He was contorting in his chair. "I got to get out of here, or it's all going to go epileptic."

"Where are we going now?" Melissa asked him.

Cosmo watched the two of them. *For what?* he asked himself. *The invisible and now broken thread between them?*

"I want to go to the Grotto," Moscow said. "I've got to get out of here." That was their other favorite haunt, a smoky blues bar that served two-dollar beers. It was the place they could straighten things out.

Moscow pulled his hair back with both hands. He seemed desperate. He needed a familiar hovel, the comfort of a known variable. Apparently, he had noticed the two falling bodies around him.

"Okay," Cosmo said.

"We'll go somewhere to talk," Moscow said across the table to Cosmos and Melissa. "It's too loud here."

On the way out, Cosmo walked on ahead. By now it was wholly dark and much cooler. Melissa walked Cooper before they went on their way. The three of them stood there in the darkness, watching the dog relieve itself. It seemed to move at its own speed. It couldn't perceive that anything could have changed between its owner and her two friends.

"We gotta get out of here," Moscow said impatiently. He then spun around and punched the side of the car with his right hand.

He swore at himself and kissed his knuckles, then, getting mad again, slapped the hood, this time with an open palm. "It's time to leave," he said quietly.

Finally, the monster convertible rolled out onto the two-lane road. They all knew the way to the Grotto. It, too, was underground. Melissa was still driving spectacularly. The only difference now was that she had removed her sunglasses. Through the rearview mirror, the new pair could now look into the dim centers of each other's eyes, which reflected, Cosmo knew, more than headlights. If he thought about it, there was something like starlight there, too, in the theoretical sense. About Moscow's eyes, though, he couldn't tell. Moscow was looking straight ahead now and said nothing. Until he started to talk about how strong he was, how much dead weight he could lift. Then he was silent again. He could be thinking of anything, Cosmo supposed, though on a cloudless night with a missing moon, knowing Moscow, he was probably thinking about his astronomy, the study of the constellations.

***

It was inexplicable why Melissa avoided her natural habitat in her automobile—the freeway. Instead, they were zipping through the dark back roads, enroute to their favorite bar. But her driving skills were unimpaired; there was no fear of accident, not with her sure and effortless eye for the wheel. The way Cosmo would remember it, they were on the blackened stretch of asphalt before they rounded a shallow bend and saw the red lights. He wouldn't have expected this to break Melissa's concentration, which had always been unflappable, but there it was. Melissa slowed down as they heard the bells from a distance. Cosmo could see the red flashes in Melissa's eyes in the mirror, even if he wasn't able to see anything for himself. The car passed the twin yellow R.'s stenciled on the center of the roadway and came to a stop in front of the railroad crossing. The impulse for anybody, for someone of Melissa's skill in particular, should have been to look left and right and then scurry across the tracks before the gates closed, signaling the train's arrival. But the car slowed to a standstill. Melissa stiffened in her seat. Her gloved hands let go of the wheel.

"We'll wait here," she said.

Moscow implored her. "Phantom warning," he said to her. "Go across the tracks, Mel. It's alright."

"No, we'll wait until it passes," she said. Cosmo had almost never heard her oppose Moscow before.

Moscow was incensed. He asked her why, what was the logical reason? Did she have some terrible experience with trains meeting head-on with cars in her past? Did she have a friend, a relative, who met with an untimely end on a night just like this one?

"No, not at all," Melissa said. "We'll just wait here." She was insistent, unmovable, a fixed object in space and time.

"I'll drive it, if you want," Cosmo offered, "if you don't want to." Cosmo was massaging Melissa's left ear discreetly, as if Moscow couldn't notice. There was compassion in his voice.

"Leave it alone, Cos," Moscow said. He was still upset. "If she doesn't want to drive, let her wait."

"Okay," Cosmo said. He was content where he was for once. It was a rare and delicious feeling. The gate closed in front of them. Now they had no choice but to wait for the train.

But the promised train didn't come. The lights continued to flash and the bells continued to sound in the night, but there was no train, no matter how far Cosmo looked into the distance left or right.

Then Moscow said, "I'll do some real reconnaissance," and stepped out of the car. Cosmo followed him across the tracks. He looked east with his hands on his hips, and then looked west with the same pose. Cosmo climbed over the gate and stood watching.

"I'll bet I can do fifty push-ups on the tracks before our ghost train pulls in," Moscow said.

"Sure you can," Cosmo replied, almost laughing. "You can't be serious."

"You'd do it too, if you had any real spine," Moscow said. His voice was just a bit malicious.

"We're not going to fight over her," Cosmo said, looking over his shoulder. "Are we?" he asked.

"Well, you're not going to stand up and be counted because it's impossible for an invertebrate to really stand up."

Cosmo looked east and then west. There was nothing except the dim parallel of the tracks meeting at a point of infinity focus in both directions. Cosmo dropped to the ground, finding two spots for his large hands on the asphalt builtup around the metal tracks.

"One," he counted out loud, raising his body off the earth. Moscow was down, too, and up in an instant. The two looked forward as they began their count.

In the background, over the bells and faint hint of the radio that still blared out of the open convertible, Melissa honked the horn. Once, then twice. A plaintive and uncomfortable sound. Cosmo wished that she'd stop. The angle of the headlights caught their moving bodies on the crossing as they strained toward the ground and back up again, casting the shadows from their feet and bodies ahead of them into the darkness.

They were counting. "Eleven, twelve, thirteen…" Neither of them was in too good a shape. One hundred push-ups was an impossible target, Cosmo knew. Fifty was more like it. But he knew he could do more than thick-middled Moscow. Cosmo would humiliate him a little and they would go on with the rest of the night and whatever that held.

The tendons wrenched in Cosmos' elbows, across his back. He heard the door of the convertible close. He sensed Melissa walking up behind him. Cosmo wondered whether someone who didn't intend something suicidal was really snuffing it. "Twenty," he said, loudly enough so that Moscow could hear.

He was thinking of Melissa, invisible behind him as they approached thirty. Moscow's face was set in the darkness. He didn't seem to notice anything around him. Beyond the din of the crossing bells, Cosmo swore he heard a line from the radio. It was an old blues song about losing love and becoming a sort of ghost. He wondered if this might not come true, whether it was a prophecy, maybe he would reach the land of the phantoms this very night.

A new and terrifyingly bright star ruptured the night sky as the heralded train turned a distant bend. Its horn blared out in the night, a perfunctory blast. Its conductor could not possibly have seen the two small obstacles in his path. Before looking up, Cosmo felt the vibrations in his chest first, conducted through the rail.

"Game's up, bright boy," he said to Moscow on his right. But Moscow wasn't listening.

The two men were up to forty push-ups. The front of the train a mile away, and they both knew it was an impossible task. The train had shattered immeasurable blackness, the locomotive exploding it in light and sound, in slow and brilliant motion. A panoply of light and accelerating metal. Sure, it was diesel and not steam, Cosmo thought, but it would do, that was certain.

But Cosmo wasn't going to budge either. If Moscow refused to move until the last possible second, neither would he. In his head, he talked to the train now, to take him away from here, to take him bodily into the sky. He meant it, like a kid praying during a lightning storm. *Take me straight up to Orion's belt*, he thought. And he knew what was coming. It was elemental, like discovering oil, or fire, that you could grow things in the earth. His eyes shook in their sockets. His world was rumbling, and curiously he wasn't as frightened as he felt he should be.

Thirty seconds to go, a half mile away, forty-five pushups, and the noise had become deafening. The train wasn't even trying to screech to an already impossible stop. Apparently, they were still hidden from whomever was behind the thundering light. Melissa yelled for them to get away. Moscow, in the last moment, looked up at Cosmo and mouthed "You lose," as the light and sound reached their maximum point, just a few seconds before impact.

Cosmo's eardrums popped as he rolled off the tracks into the gravel bed. He was raked by rocks. He felt swift, sure hands lift and pull his body from behind. He was cut away from Moscow, whom he saw moving forward, insect-like, across the tracks, in the opposite direction. They were cut away from each other by a rush of metal and rolling darkness, annihilating speed, a cataclysm of sound that smashed everything with a truly incalculable power. Cosmo thought of parachuting, without the chute, of course, a plunge into thick burgeoning air, end over end over end. At the moment of potential collision, Melissa had screamed in a low, terrible voice. She screamed for the both of them, though they were, out of self-preservation, silent and concerned with escape. *Remember*, Cosmo told himself, *she was the honest one among them.*

He felt no longer bound by physical laws, in freefall, after the engine cut out and the aircraft was subject to its own treatises on motion. He probably needed Moscow to explain the physics of the moment.

He nearly collapsed into Melissa's arms. He had rolled over and over in a kind of military maneuver. Now he could feel her flesh underneath her blouse through his shirt. This soft contact was his reward. Despite the cool air, they were both soaked from inside. He smelled creosote, dust, faint perfume, the musk of her leather jacket, the scent of wine on her lips.

The clatter of the train was impossible to face while standing. Cosmo and Melissa hobbled and fell to their knees in the grass by the car. By some miracle, Cooper had jumped out of the back of the convertible and stood in the darkness, stunned and confused and now motionless. Only Cooper's eyes, with their dull animal glow, a glow made almost supernatural by the red flashing lights, showed that the dog was still breathing. The eyes behind them worried Cosmo more than anything else.

He couldn't know then whether Moscow had been thrown high into the night air, but Cosmo was sure that he had not been caught gruesomely under the wheels. If he were safe, Moscow would probably be laughing, flat on his back very likely, and looking up at the stars, letting it roar, just from the adrenaline or the stupidity of it all. Cosmos and Melissa looked on, hands barely touching, as the darkness of the endless train separated them from an even darker night and the body of their unconscious friend.

Cathedral Street

Love for you was always a sort of religion. It was always something to cherish in dark rooms, with your secrets folded and warmed next to the body. You said her name quietly, like an incantation against evil, and the mantra always succeeded. You always convinced yourself that she heard you there, a child in the dark, murmuring a prayer. You assured yourself that she heard and believed in your formidable sense of faith, though like yourself, she had no proof, no image of a smiling face captured on a towel. You wrote notes in silence by candlelight, in the catacomb of your pure desire; you shaped the vowels in her name; that was all you dared in measurable speech. You told no one. You scratched at night in a secret diary that gave no relief. You earned nothing, sacrificed nothing, and risked very little. Yet your loss was immense, greater than the night that disguised you from the delicate flame of her breath, the bloom of her face, her thin arms, the set of her shoulders in her sundress worn haphazardly at evening. You forgot so much. So much to remind you of, here in the desert, the highway you plod.

***

Your name is Maxwell, if that could indeed distinguish you. Tonight, you don't feel individual. That dome of stars, this highway, its monotonous headlights, the pale-yellow lines, they're here to erase you, to let thought wander. The highway tonight is empty, and that adds solace to your trek, your pilgrimage to the middle of the state, to the edge of the forest, for a truth, for a partial truth perhaps. Her surname was Appleby, now it's Jones. Her first name continues to be Sarah. Her new daughter is named Melissa. Her husband, you remember his hulking good looks at the wedding, a Clark Gable, the attorney, you'd like to forget. These new alliances, these unbelievable forces, these facts. She expects you at her home to explain to you. You don't know what to say. You will not think of this. Or try not to.

The towns go by on their green placards, edged by jewels caught in your headlights.

***

Once she was an unbreakable habit, something unalterable in your personal makeup, a chemical that you craved with a kind of addiction. You looked into her blue eyes and thought of miracles, of lakes, of the spring water that carved its flood mark on the rocks around the lake. She was that mark of terrible, high water. You took the canoe to the island and waded out in the warm summer muck, two pairs of bare feet lapped by bathwater. You walked on the island, knowing no one else was there. No one else could witness when she told you that yes, you were the one. How you held her, how extravagant that kiss. Even that was unalterable. She whispered your name in the sunlight and some part of you quickened into a dance of life, like the butterflies around you. Some part of you promised her that you could love her forever. The waters back to the other side of the lake, to dull civilization were a mirror that coaxed two silhouettes back up to the blue sky, an imago you both could never forget. Memory is like that, a cul-de-sac for people and objects locked accidentally into configurations that only seem unchangeable. What could you say but yes when she promised?

Refusing, she might have drowned right then. What would any decent person manage there in the high summer grass?

***

Choose me, you tell the highway, this night, because it can be no other. You are used to running away. You ran from her that summer. Now you can tell the truth in person. It only seems too late, but is it? You press on the gas and ease into the passing lane. A truck with anonymous cargo blocks your progress. This particular problem is easily solved, a simple sum of physical forces.

Then, you think, you were all ghosts, living and breathing in darkness, characters in a film you at once watched and photographed. Everything seemed unreal then, a fantasy of summer, of unbelievable circumstance.

But tonight, it's different. Surely it is. Tonight, that fraction of thought that blossoms into deed seems even more perfectible. This is the night (you tell yourself, tuning the radio) that Hamlet figures everything out, and it doesn't take a duel to pull the words from his tongue. This is the night when Prufrock, in sunglasses, rides shotgun next to his shining bride, in his convertible, into an endless sunset. He's going to the beach, fast, to watch the surf crash on the rocks and the sun dip itself into a roiling summer sea.

***

For years you fell out of touch, no letters or phone calls. Maxwell and Sarah pining away in different cities, hearing through friends of each other's forays into business, politics. She learned, of all things, to sell precious stones. She had a knack for management. All this, and from comparative literature. What else can you do, she told you then, except find something else to do, something useful. You chuckled, agreeing, drunk with love, with margaritas on her couch in her apartment. You watched her eyes as she spoke to you and thought of some kind of inexplicable gems. Even then the metaphor worked itself hollow.

***

The first months were the months of withdrawal. In self-pity, you asked yourself what was it like when Adam first worked outside the garden? Was he worse off for having seen perfection, or did it give him something to strive for? Did he think he could win it back through strenuous effort, through dedication, tilling the soil?

Darkness was your companion, your most intimate acquaintance. You'd been cut off. You'd been had. Your friends understood. They could sit and tell you the truth for hours, but did it sink in? Did you choose to believe it? They'd like to think so. They'd like to sit and decide for you. They'd like to coerce the lie of the mind that weaves in and out of night. What you needed most was fever, that fiery headache that mixes people and things that never ever could have met in daylight but who meet again and again under the cover of delirium. Then you'd twist in the blanket, begging her face to dissipate, to recede with a low tide back from where this new and old version of her came from. You were sure, in your achy freedom, that this had to do with moonlight, with its pull on all our waters. After all, blood is only a poor substitute for seawater. Surely, moonlight caused this oscillation, this flux in elemental fluid. Who can say for sure? Wouldn't we be better off with the starfish's dreams? Instead, you toss and turn in the oncoming tide, defenseless, your five limbs searching for an anchor, a bit of rock to focus on. You ask yourself, is this a desperate man's request? Is this too much to ask?

***

Something is washed up on the sand; you can make out its oblong form in the dimness. It's some kind of crate. On more detailed inspection—

some kind of chest. You will not dare to hope for treasure. There is the past, all barnacles and rusting hinges, but the raw form of its container solid and firm, and who knows what capacity? In this nightscape, in the dream, you are forced to open it, to dirty your hands on its rough surface—curious how it isn't locked, but it takes such effort to pry it open, to lift and understand this burden which has been delivered so carelessly, so purposefully, by the waves.

As you open it, you plunge headlong into its gaping jaws, head over heels, dizzied with the force of gravity that draws you down. You never knew you carried such great weight, such mass in your bones. You rush past the walls of the labyrinth, reaching out for roots, for any kind of bracken or rocks that might slow your tumble. It's impossible, of course. There is no terminal velocity, no maximum distance to fall. It's one miracle after another, the night is calling out to you. You look over your shoulder as you plunge and see the moon staring yellow and full back at you, a Cyclops of desire and knowing. What riddles that face holds, if you only had a moment to ponder it. If you could only slow the camera down to one frame at a time. You would gain such clarity on what comprises movement. Muybridge, that pornographer of motion, his horses, his naked running men, one heaving muscle at a time would have nothing on you. You would become an expert on moving people and things through the ether of time. You might smile at the force of your discovery. But not now. Now there is only the icy rush of damp across your cheeks, the heat of re-entry on the back of your spine, the confusion of physical revolution through the void. There you go, and ever more quickly. You don't know what to say. You couldn't explain yourself if someone asked. How are you going to reason hitting the ground with such intensity? Impact is likely to be spectacular. It becomes so dark that you add invisibility to your traits as a bullet. You hope finally, for pure blue water, for a cushion, a landing pad. Like a cliff diver. Certainly your treasure chest can hold only so much night. You're hoping for such logic and then suddenly you bolt up in your bed, spattering sweat across the walls as your dream body splutters its contents across an unbroken lake, a perfect blue pane as solid as asphalt but more glamorous, more willing to show back what it's given, less self-assured. Closer to invisibility, to that pleasure of nothingness the fevered self so passionately craves.

***

Her house is set back away from the asphalt, disguised by a few conifers. It doesn't appear to be trying to be anything remarkable. The ground is covered with leaves. There seems to be a space for your rented Avis. You rock your car back and forth tentatively into position. You decide whether to lock your door. There doesn't appear to be any danger. You hear rustling behind you. There is a moment of panicked rage. You would like to be off into the woods, across the dark and limitless terrain.

"Max?" a voice asks behind you. You decide not to lock the car after all.

"Sarah?" you ask in return. Surely this is the most uncertain of meetings.

You turn, smiling.

She is standing in front of you, holding a small girl with short blonde hair in her arms, who is perhaps only pretending to be asleep. The child has a thumb in her mouth, her delicate arm positioned as if sculpted out a light material, a light batik. So perfect the set of her tiny limbs.

You kiss Sarah on her left cheek, the side of her face unprotected by her child. You notice the two of them are wearing identical blue jackets.

"It's good to see you again," she offers.

"Yes, it is." There is no time for thinking now. All this can only be unrehearsed, rudely improvised.

You carry your overnight bag from your trunk, while Sarah carries Melissa, who hasn't yet stirred.

"My car? Is it okay?" you ask.

"It's fine, don't sweat it," she says. "Trevor will be home from the office late," she adds. "Very late."

"Right," you say. You didn't want to meet Trevor anyway. Not until later. This is no time to worry.

One thought as she opens the door for you: all children are profoundly beautiful. Melissa walks sleepily and quickly to her room, playing shy.

"She's a princess," you tell Sarah. You both discern this as a truth.

"It's great to see you," you say now that you are alone.

"Yes, yes it is," she says, taking off her coat. She looks fuller, the hall light sculpts her face differently than you remember it. But, yes, profoundly beautiful.

"We'll have dinner, now, I think," she says, accepting your bottle of wine.

"Yes, that would be good," you say. I am so happy to be here, you think to yourself, silent and alarmed at the strength of the feeling.

***

Suburban dangers: Lyme disease, the fear of depreciation, the rude materialism of shopping malls. Don't forget solitude, you tell yourself. You kissed her hello on a warm cheek. She moved a hand through her short, dark hair. She saw you looking at her.

"Its natural color," she told you later, before you asked. You rhapsodized once about her blonde hair, but it doesn't matter. She looks even more perfected, more comfortable, fulfilled.

Hello. How fine this recognition.

***

Suddenly, there is dinner, after the greeting, after she takes you in again, into her shelter.

"Are you tired, Max?" You are eating a salad with a three-tined, silver fork. And it is delicious. "Was it difficult?" she asks. "The trip up here?"

"Not at all," you hear yourself saying. A few hours of driving, of near darkness. The highway wasn't crowded. You are careful to talk between mouthfuls. You feel disoriented, like you are wearing someone else's clothes which are uncomfortably sized.

"Traffic was light?"

"Yes, very. Nothing in the way coming here. Nothing at all."

Surely she's radiant as she takes away the salad dishes. Dinner will be stewed rabbit. Exotic chicken, you'll pretend. She's so certain of her movements around her dining room. She sets the place in front of her despite your protestations, like a noble setting a table for a good friend who's returned from a pilgrimage from the Holy Land. Sure, you think, that's it exactly. She doesn't seem to be herself. Not at all.

The talk turns inevitably to business.

"So, what do you market these days?"

You imagine she pauses for a moment, nearly embarrassed. There is the tiniest glitch in her well-rehearsed motions around the living room, those small arcs of her fork from her plate to her mouth.

"Well, recently, diamonds, actually."

"Diamonds?" you say.

"Yes, and the usual semi-precious gems."

She smiles and turns away. You recognize with pain her throaty chuckle, that mischievous laughter that held up the world for ridicule in your dreams.

"Well, I try to tell myself that diamonds do come from South Africa. But they are double commission!"

You are laughing like old friends, now. You could tell her everything, if you had the inkling and the time.

"Do you like rabbit?" she asks you.

"Yes, I haven't had it in years," you say.

"I suppose you're still able to be pure in the city," she says, laughing.

"Oh, that's it exactly," you say.

Despite yourself, you admit her new life agrees with her, gloriously. Her politics were once so volatile, so militant. She took up the barricade so often, so completely, and now this mode, this suburban mode so incapable of the passion of the trenches. But then there she is, rocking Melissa to sleep in her arms, and you think of Raphael's

Madonnas, that simplicity of feeling, even when stylized. She tells you you wouldn't understand; you wouldn't fathom this complexity, the pure experience she had in creating all this, her new life.

You dread meeting her husband, an attorney, the erstwhile performance artist.

It could be an evening of great difficulty, or hope. You'll have to decide.

***

She lights a fire with a real log of oak in the fireplace. You are sitting across from each other, like two comfortable old chums, she on a white couch, you on an easy chair done in red leather, trying its best to be distinguished.

When you were Melissa's age, you tell her, you were always the first one to be hypnotized by fire, to kiss its golden fingers, hands you could only dare to shake.

She smiles for you. It's your knack for the comfort of memory, of recalling a child's genius. You're still appreciated.

Sarah moves her head away from the door, to hear it. The wind is assembling something outside, some kind of autumn storm, nothing extravagant, only wind and cold rain.

"I wish Trevor would call," she tells herself out loud. "I think it is going to rain," she adds.

She excuses herself and goes to the other room to telephone.

***

It rained once, long ago. You both held a drink on the couch in her parents' empty house. She was twenty-one. How old were you? She had just shown you the one poem by Baudelaire that she thought wasn't pompous. The poet goes to the grave of his dead wife, someone he probably didn't give much thought to while she was still breathing.

Genuine emotion, she said. You agreed. She read you French and you poured her another drink, this night it was something with Kahlua, its sticky-sweetness coating your tongue and teeth.

Outside there was summer lightning, a huge flashing street sign, signifying rain. She moved over to the window. You looked on gloriously, like watching a dance. She opened it wide; the wind pushed the hair off her face.

"I love lightning," she said.

Again, you agreed. The rain came in sporadic splashes at first, then in torrents. She took a minute or two to decide to close the window. When she did, her face was wet and smiling. She looked distant and content, gazing off across the dim summer sky punctuated by lightning and thunder. She closed the window halfway and turned toward the couch and sat down. You looked at one another as if something important had transpired between you. You took her hands and kissed them. She smelled of summer sweat, perfume, and Kahlua, that elegant liqueur.

An immensely fat dog wallowed into the room, an ancient Labrador, graying around its edges, its splayed feet moving tentatively. Its head was down, uncertain of interrupting.

"Puma!" she exclaimed, breaking the embrace. And you weren't sorry, given her outburst of care for this dog.

"Is Puma scared of the rain?" she asked the dog. Its thick tail managed a single wag. She held the dog to her, and its face brightened. It put its tongue back in its mouth. There you were, the three of you in the near darkness, hearing the booms in the night. The dog looked up periodically for reassurance. She held it tightly. You both nodded to each other. How happy each creature in that room despite heavy weather.

***

"Trevor was just leaving," she tells you. "He'll be back in under an hour."

"Wonderful," you say. The flames are quiet yellow embers, incapable of their former powers.

It would be good to sit and reminisce and watch everything turn to warm ash.

Melissa came in at one point and hugged her mother good night.

"Honey, this is Max," Sarah told you and her.

She had to be coaxed into looking at you.

"He's tall," Melissa told her mother, quite conspiratorially, in a little, knowing voice.

"Yes, he is," Sarah nodded back.

You are over six feet, it's true, almost a foot taller than Sarah. It's an odd thing to say, you think to yourself.

"Say goodnight to Max," Sarah admonishes.

"Goodnight, Mister Max."

Melissa has her mother's startling blue eyes. Of course, all children's eyes seem lighter, as if cosmetically altered. Time turns them to their real shade, you think.

You watch Melissa trek off into the hallway. Sarah follows her to tuck her in.

All children are beautiful, you remind yourself. It doesn't wear thin for you. How could it now?

***

"Trevor, honey, this is Max, Max Edmonds."

Sarah points you out as if you stood in a crowd and needed discovering.

You shake a firm hand, a lawyer's hand, sure of its business.

"How do you do?" Trevor says to you. His British accent is superb, you think. They met in Cambridge, you remember. He reminded her of Cary Grant, his bumbling elegance. He played in a rock-and-roll band, a drummer, and quoted Keats. He works in a middle-sized firm and makes an excellent salary. You envy him his ability to assume his character without acting. He is completely natural. Without a thought, himself. It's wonderful.

"I met you at your wedding," you remind him.

"Yes, of course," he says. His brow comes together under his thick black hair, just for a second. He doesn't remember.

Sarah and Trevor stand for a moment together, a happy couple, and they are an exquisite match. No one could deny it. No one. There can be nothing to regret, you tell yourself. They have re-formed their alliance around you, despite you, in fact. Not touching, but powerfully connected. You almost shudder from the force of it. It's unbelievable, its strength.

"How's Melissa?" Trevor asks her under his breath.

You weren't supposed to hear that. Yet you're confident, despite all exterior signs, that you should be here, if only to see them together, in their humble perfection, there, like this. In front of you.

"I'll go check on her," Trevor says, "and then I think I'll turn in."

Sarah says she'll show me to the guest room.

"Good to meet you again," Trevor offers.

"Sure it is," you reply. You all shake hands good night as she shows you to your bed.

***

A few seconds in the near dark, and your head swims, inexplicably, into sadness.

How soon the body forgets its one fever, how it protects itself from such fire, such blindness, such fury trained on the soul. You never forgot your past with her. You never consciously tried to forget, but the body, its ignorant lust for survival found that numbing river where it would not have to work to remember, the forgetful slumber of the routine. You fall asleep listening for the wind, stray pillow talk from the two of them an entire floor above you, or just maybe the comfortable snores of a child.

***

She knocks on your door on Saturday morning to wake you up. Trevor left before you, back to his endless work in the office. Melissa watches cartoons exploding on the largest TV you remember seeing in a real home in the kitchen. She and Sarah eat pancakes you yourself make.

They are laughing quietly together, mother and daughter at the absurd violence of cats and dogs on the screen. Between mouthfuls of flapjacks and syrup, they look at the screen non-commitally, not really interested. You watch them, unnoticed, from the pantry, wiping dishes with a blue terry cloth towel.

"Thanks for breakfast," she says to you. "Delicious."

"You're very welcome," you say with mock seriousness.

"Melissa has an idea," she says. Melissa looks up past her plate and the TV to you, looking you up and down with just a bit of suspicion.

"She has a plan," Sarah suggests.

Melissa goes back to her cartoons, ignoring you both. A child of invincible concentration, you think.

"Tell your plan to Max," Sarah continues. For some reason, she wants Melissa to like you, or at least to acknowledge your presence in the room.

Melissa stuffs her mouth full of pancake and manages, with surprising diction given the volume of food, to mumble that she wants to go to the park.

"To the dolphins," she says.

"The aquarium?" you ask her, wondering.

"No, not real fish. Metal," Melissa says.

Sarah explains the park has dolphins to ride on, like rocking horses, and swing sets, which Melissa loves to play on.

"The swings!" Melissa manages between her food and a commercial.

"To the dolphins!" you tell both of them, going for Melissa's empty dish.

You're surprised by your own enthusiasm for such simple things.

***

The park is suburban, immaculately maintained, even this late in autumn. It's tree-lined and new. Though it's Saturday and not too chilly, there are only a few joggers and people race-walking. There are no other children in the park. Melissa heads straight for the swing set. Sarah lets you push Melissa back and forth carefully. She wants to lunge higher and higher. You notice Melissa's breath in the cold, her cheeks puffing as she strains against the pendulum of gravity that she would so love to transcend.

"Higher, higher!" she tells you.

You wouldn't dare to be anything but careful. There you are: Sarah, her daughter, yourself. The alignment seems unalterable. Sarah smiles at you, knowing that Melissa is in good hands. You're able to persuade Melissa to take a breather; your back aches.

"Thanks, Max," Melissa says, running toward the dolphins on the other side of the field.

"She can handle herself?" you ask Sarah.

"I'll watch her, of course, but I think so," she says.

"Already in control of herself," you suggest.

"That's true," Sarah says.

"A princess, you say. Truly precocious."

"Must be Trevor's side of the family," she speculates.

"I doubt it," you say. Sarah is a bit flattered. "A little lady," you add.

Melissa is riding a dolphin, and you're watching the rhythm of Sarah's breath in the cold, its easy intake and exhalation of the pure air. You three know that nothing could rob you of this moment together, its simple inevitability.

***

Back at the homestead, Melissa begs off again into the house.

"Goodbye Mister Max," she says to you before scampering away.

"Good, Melissa," Sarah says. "Melissa likes you," she continues. But she sounds unconvinced.

You are left there alone, the two of you, to say goodbye.

"You should stay for dinner," Sarah suggests.

"I have to get back tonight. A concert in the city. I must go," you say. "I'm writing a review."

She nods and you understand one another perfectly.

Years ago, you kissed goodnight in the darkness, and it was the moment that could have meant something else. That was one goodbye. Now you feel her solid weight, her measurable strength. You sense her happiness, how eager she is to show you that she is happy.

You hold her in your arms for a moment under the sky, an embrace of lost relatives more than lovers. You say goodbye. You are overjoyed at seeing her. Though her hair had changed color, her body carries its original form. Her laugh thrills you. For a moment, you think everything, all this between you, is surmountable. The rude current of time might, after all of this, still be navigable. A ride through a narrow canyon, the raft of yourself grazing the rocks that provide whitewater, but still traversable. At least you can make it from one end to the other.

How could you not know, looking back now, at the pattern in her eyes, the way she told you goodbye that night long ago. What magic! You would be lucky to hear of such a love once in a lifetime. And it was your own, certainly. You held each other on days like these and thought of a perfection so rarely allotted to mortals.

Leaving, you hear the leaves under your wheels. You tap your horn on the way out, politely, as if warning a cab of your presence on a busy street. You wave to each other until the trees between you are too thick. Once again, you approximate what's invisible to one another. But you know you have each other beyond the trees.

***

That night, you go to the concert, really your first love and your most steadfast, into the world of the cathedral turned stage. The space in the cathedral is large, on a medieval scale, when twenty thousand craftsmen labored for fifty years to sculpt a building, to paint a dome, to buttress a structure on all sides with stone. You think of the labor of ants that could build a pyramid, stone upon seamless stone, given enough determined energy and the will to see a cathedral rise out of the cold ground, the kind of conversion of Constantine, the fiery cross in the sky that could turn armies. It's this kind of commitment of the madman, the heretic, the saint, all crusaders for a vision.

In the dark, vast space, the ensemble of performers gathers slowly, moving across the warm circle carved by the spotlights in this space of contemplation, of right thinking. The echoes multiply, bifurcate, divide, and suffuse the nave, the transept. The music builds slowly, a headache you don't at first mark, a quiet mounting climax; before you know it, you are one with your lover and a third of the way to that thunderous sundering with the present into that tumultuous annihilation of the self that you crave. You recall a musicologist who wrote that anything that behaves like a motive is a motive, a repetitive figure, a building block, a piece of the architecture around you. This music, he wrote you, pares the intricacies of music to an intimate vocabulary, its essential skeleton, a repeatable and inevitable progression of chords, each a tiny castle for the ear. The wash of the sonic explosion becomes clear to you when the first piece ends, the tingle from the center of the spine, shivering your frame for you. It's true; it's exquisite.

You think, if only for a moment, this public experience has been staged for your benefit, for your individual elucidation, for emergences of the soul, minute and paramount crises only you can sense and attempt to explain. Not to dismiss this confrontation with the self, the id, with its ravenous twistings and turnings in your moist pew. You remember her face in the darkness, her voice most of all. You think for a moment of a bright membrane of the soul, which dictates what truths lie silent and imminent, humbly transcendent, behind the delicate, colored shadows on the cathedral's north wall. The music is only a fabrication, a honing of those sounds that please you, that pull you by the ear again and again to whisper and reassure you here in the dark. It would not be difficult to fabricate these nearly invisible, wise shadows articulated here under the dome. You couldn't invent this grandeur. And now that it's conjured, you can't explain it away.

Afterward, when it is all over, you walk out of one darkness to another, head bowed, into the night air, to your silent vehicle.

***

On the way home, driving your rental back to its own, you listen to more music and think to yourself, *How many people have died adjusting their car radios?*

Words for a Mood

He would like to say that he had been a good father. He had his failings, sometimes he fell down, but everyone did, and he would want her to know that. Felice had changed her phone number again. When Mr. Stiers called London, he heard a recorded message saying that the number was no longer connected. He called her law firm, which acted as mediator in such situations. When he did, a gruff voice told him he knew nothing about his daughter. Perhaps the case was handled by someone else in the firm; the British voice claimed to know nothing.

"My name is Stiers, Ryan Stiers," he said. "I am her father."

"Please do not call again, Mr. Stiers," the attorney said, relenting a little. "I am authorized by my client to say that she is alive and healthy, but she does not wish to speak with any of her relatives."

"I only want to talk to her," Mr. Stiers pleaded. He knew it would do no good to argue, but he tried anyway. The attorney refused to divulge anything further.

"If you do see your client," Mr. Stiers said finally, "if you see Felice, please tell her that I called."

"I will," the attorney said. "But she does not wish to speak with anyone from her family," the voice said with professional obligation.

"Give her my love," Stiers added, a bit defeated and embarrassed, really, as the man on the other line hung up. He felt the weight of the phone in his hand and tapped it gently in his other palm before placing it back in its cradle. Mr. Stiers found himself thinking about when he had last seen his prodigal daughter. It annoyed him that he didn't really know without resorting to mental arithmetic. It was almost five years ago that his only daughter had walked through the door right there in this very same apartment. Felice had been wearing an ermine sable, high heels, and smelled of perfume. Her hair was lighter than he'd remembered. She spoke carefully and kissed him hello. Only later did he realize how cool her manner to him had really been. Because it was Thanksgiving, everyone was much too occupied then with other things to worry about it.

Right now, Mr. Stiers was a bit overcome. It was five years later, and because he was flying the next morning on business, he wanted to see if his daughter was ready to see him again. He had a nagging sense that he had embarrassed himself on the phone, but it was already 7:30 and he had to get to his office early in order to get ready for his trip.

He wondered if anyone suspected that he wasn't by nature a punctual person, that it really did take a certain discipline. He was always careful not to demand punctuality in other people, though it did annoy him to be stuck at a meeting waiting for that critical person who would fulfill a committee's quorum while he sat trying hard not to look at his watch, sipping his water and going over his presentation to the others seated around the table. He hated that kind of waiting. He hated the loss of control. The thought now of going to see Felice without her knowing he was coming was almost alarming. He didn't know if he could bring himself to do it. He told himself it was no time to worry and got his things together for his day. He was having lunch with Elmeyer, an old friend who also had difficulties with his sons and daughters. But Elmeyer was a psychologist, too, and Mr. Stiers wasn't sure whether that hurt or helped.

Locking his door, only the bottom lock because the housekeeper would be by to clean today since it was a Thursday, he thought that probably it didn't help, but he reminded himself to be sure to ask his friend anyway if the chance came up.

***

They had gone to school together in what seemed a different time altogether, though Mr. Stiers was only sixty-five, sill in excellent shape, and apt to live to be a hundred as anyone, whenever he thought about it.

The restaurant was next to his office and only a few blocks from the hotel where Dr. Mahler Elmeyer, Psy. D. was staying. He was in town to present a paper at the medical school, something about a rare disorder in patients with the two halves of the brain severed.

"No words for emotional states," Mahler said. "The left brain does the words, the right brain does the emotions," he explained between mouthfuls of soup. "But when the two are separated, there are all kinds of problems—ulcers, heart attacks, even respiratory failure."

Mahler was a man who, despite a possible intellectual past, which made Stiers immediately suspicious, seemed to enjoy life a great deal. Mahler was bald in the way of men whose hair disappears at thirty and they never miss it. The energy they saved worrying translated into deeds done in the world, it seemed to Stiers. His own hair was completely gray, but he still had a good deal of it, and secretly, he would admit it as a small source of pride, though he would have perhaps found it a kind of vanity in someone else.

Mahler was stocky, well-exercised, and ruddy faced. He had a shrink's requisite beard but despite his affinity for books had never worn glasses. When the two men played squash, which they would have done this time had Mahler's knees not been hurting him, Mahler was the power player who swatted the ball around with wristy, pummeling strokes, while Stiers was the traditionalist, knees gracefully bent a little, meeting the ball at just the right point in his stance, who would win most every game. At lunch, Mahler ordered a Scotch while Stiers ordered a glass of wine.

"And how is Alice?" Mahler asked.

"She's fine," Stiers replied. Alice was at work, too. She worked as an assistant to a curator downtown. During the past week, she was in Los Angeles, doing publicity for a show. After the divorce years ago, with Felice's mother, Alice and Stiers never married, though they had shared their lives for almost twelve years now. It always surprised people that Stiers dispensed with such a necessary convention. Maybe it was because he seemed like such an example from an older school, which was in some ways undoubtedly true, but Stiers still proved himself difficult to measure at times. And Elmeyer, though he had remained married for thirty years to the same woman, seemed to appreciate the unconventional conventionality in his friend. This contrast was one thing that kept up their interest in maintaining their friendship over the years, Stiers thought.

Finally, after they had dispensed with their food and Mahler offered Stiers a cigar, Stiers found the right opening.

"Your daughter is engaged now?" Stiers asked.

"Oh yes, my better half must have written you," Mahler replied.

"She went to Princeton, I remember."

"Economics. Phi Beta Kappa. We're very proud of her."

Stiers took a deep breath and began.

"I wish my daughter had gone to college. She left home and met a wealthy man from the Middle East."

"You never mention her anymore," Mahler continued. "Is she alright? Paris, right, or Madrid or something. She's doing well?"

"I think so," Stiers said, "though we haven't spoken in quite a few years."

"That's unfortunate," Mahler said. He paused and his brow knit itself together. Stiers thought that he might put on the mask of his profession, but he didn't really. Mahler just looked back at his friend with open eyes and said, "We all must learn to live on our own."

"I know that," Stiers replied. He was thinking about what it would be like to drive in a cab to Felice's apartment. It would probably be raining out. He would have to give the cabby the address, not knowing exactly where she lived. The cabby would be difficult and in his Cockney accent would ask about who he was visiting perhaps, and Stiers would be forced to be reticent. Taking his embarrassment for haughtiness, the cabby would give him a hard time, probably pretending to get lost in the rain. Then, finally, arriving at the address, Stiers would have to nod his assent, that, yes, this was the right building, even though he had no idea, especially since it would no doubt be dark and drizzling. And he would be deposited alone, feeling cheated by the cabby, feeling jet-lagged and tired. Then he would have to pretend that he knew what he was doing, to go to the building and ask the concierge if his daughter was in, and whether or not he should ask to see her. Probably he wouldn't, though. Just seeing where she lived and that someone was living in her apartment would be assurance enough that she was okay. He would drop off a letter, certainly, leave it with the concierge, perhaps. He would write the letter on the way over on the plane. He always wrote letters, eschewing a laptop computer for a fountain pen, which no doubt would draw distracted glances from whomever his seatmate was. But he would write a letter, telling her in a few sentences everything, that now would be a good time to clear the air between them. As for the business with the attorneys, Stiers believed it was Gregory, Felice's lover, who had put her up to it. And besides, when she saw him in the flesh, how could she not want to talk to him?

If she had learned to stand on her own two feet, what more could he ask from her? He just wanted her to know that he would still be there for her whenever she might need it. It was that simple, he thought.

Mahler said that his psychological paper was to be delivered that evening. "Alexithymia," he said, citing the technical term, "No words for mood."

Probably it's Greek, Stiers thought to himself, wondering if he should venture it. Mahler had finished smoking. He was no longer smiling, looking like he expected an answer to something that had been raised between them, two aging friends.

"I imagine it can kill a person," Stiers said finally.

"Do you want to know what I think?" Mahler asked.

Stiers nodded, unsure if he did.

"I know it can," Mahler said.

***

When Mr. Stiers thought about it, despite its ordinary physics, human flight was still a mystery to him. He could never get over the apparent impossibilities involved, the plane like a huge bumblebee could not possibly fly, even mathematically, could it? Though he knew that its mathematics was the only reason it could. That one looked at a bee and thought about flight was the most natural thing in the world. Only the physicists suggested otherwise. When he looked at his plane nuzzling the exit ramp, stolid and impersonal and most of all, very, very heavy, he thought only of dead weight that no amount of aerodynamics could redeem, and though he was trained as an engineer—many, many years ago—it still didn't prepare him for sitting in its insides and pretending to browse through a magazine like this, believing, like everybody else did, in the apparently impossible. In not-too-distant days, Mr. Stiers remembered the propeller planes, which started their engines one by one on opposite sides of the cabin, the building revolutions phasing-in and phasing-out, a rumbling crescendo. At least then, Mr. Stiers thought, the technology admitted what it was trying so hard to accomplish.

At times like these, he would remember other business trips, when Felice's mother brought her to the airport to say goodbye and he would have tried to get a window seat on the side of the plane that faced the concourse. He would wave from the outdoor ramp and then from his seat as he taxied away. Once, when Felice was still a gawky ten-year-old dressed in a red jumper suit, she and her mother stood on the outdoor observation deck and waved him away. Because of a confluence in the trajectory of propellers and the layout of the airport, he actually could make out his daughter's red form, a dash of color discernible against the dull gray concrete as his plane lumbered by, with him quite cognizant of how magical this feat must have really seemed to her.

But now Mr. Stiers concentrated on his magazine. He had a window seat, which he knew to be less comfortable physically, but reassuring somehow because he could remind himself at any time of where he actually was. It was all too simple nowadays, Mr. Stiers thought to himself as the plane powered itself into the air, people were transported as far away as they liked. He, on the other hand, respected physical distance.

Everyone was just a few hours away. Everyone took the impossible for granted, that they could sleep, eat, and write letters like this while seated on a plane moving at such a speed. When he thought like this, Mr. Stiers suspected he perhaps sounded a bit old, and promptly changed the subject of his thoughts.

But Felice's world was even smaller, Mr. Stiers continued thinking unavoidably. He knew her friend Gregory had real estate holdings in Los Angeles, Chicago, and Jordan. She was probably used to being whisked away to a new location. She was selling real estate herself, too, he knew. Perhaps she was successful at it; he had no idea. He would like to think that his daughter would be good at whatever she chose to do.

Midway over the ocean now, Mr. Stiers wrote his letter.

Dear Felice, he began with his fountain pen, *I am writing this to tell you.*

But what was he trying to tell her really?

I am writing this to tell you that I am still your father.

He went on to explain why the note would be delivered by hand, that he had assumed she had received his other letters, since they were not returned in the mail. It was only a few lines long, but it was heartfelt, he thought.

***

London was five hours off—he felt that it was even more off for him. On short trips like this one, his body felt punished by the changes in time zones. He got his luggage—a single leather valise—cleared customs, and took a taxi to his hotel room, which was a small and cramped affair, despite a certain near-luxury.

He had his meeting early the next day with very important clients who needed (as his boss had put it) their hands held throughout the deal, which was a bond transaction. The clients, there were three of them, proved to be, finally, Eton chaps whose manner put Mr. Stiers immediately at ease. The larger man, the account manager of the firm it turned out, was a tall, sunburned looking fellow, who in the chinks left for polite conversation proved quite friendly. If the whole meeting were an edifice constructed of the bricks of statistics and interest rates and the numbers of arbitrage, then it was mortared with Old World custom and a polite sense of assurance that Mr. Stiers could handily reciprocate. The deal was a sure thing, these three men opposite him around the table reassured him. And Mr. Stiers knew that he could leave them with a sense of confidence, too. It wasn't so much a sense of cockiness on his part, but he saw immediately that the variables present in this current transaction ensured success, that those higher up than himself and these men in the room were hard-set to sign the deal, and his instincts told him that he was right in this.

Mr. Stiers left after three hours of exchanging proposals, not exactly with their signature on the dotted line—that was left to their superiors to finalize—but he did leave with three firm handshakes of gentlemen like himself, which were every bit as binding as a formal contract on paper.

Normally, in the evening on a trip like this, Mr. Stiers would treat himself to a polite celebration of his small victory, a quiet dinner by himself in a restaurant of his choice, a bottle of wine which he might drink all of if he weren't careful. Although Mr. Stiers had no wine collection to speak of, he knew something of wines himself and could converse easily with friends on the subject.

He would sip his drink, order a modest three-course dinner, and go over the accomplishments the day's events had rendered to him. But Mr. Stiers wasn't as happy as he should have been. Something was bothering him, and he knew, perhaps, what it was. He kept thinking of a New Year's Eve dinner he'd had with Alice soon after they had met. They were very much in love—his first real relationship after the breakup with his first wife. This all was before he, Alice, and Felice had started to fight with one another. That last night of that year, Mr. Stiers had noticed an attractively groomed woman in a business suit. It was still a novel idea then that a businesswoman should wear such a suit and travel unaccompanied, alone, especially on New Year's Eve.

Mr. Stiers didn't care much about that, however. It was the woman's persistent and very abstemious nature that made him notice her, the way she ate her meal carefully, chewing, measuring each bite, as though half-expecting to find a bone in each mouthful. It was the way she sipped her single glass of white wine, rationing it out, he noticed, for the duration of her dinner. And although Mr. Stiers was still in the throes of watching Alice, drinking in her eyes and everything she uttered, he also couldn't help but notice the woman's sad look as the New Year turned. Then he remembered raising a full glass, toasting first Alice and then, without thinking almost, to the woman who faced him two tables away. Alice actually turned in her seat to look at her amid the mayhem of the New Year, and Mr. Stiers felt embarrassed at disturbing the moment for her.

The woman in the suit remained silent, merely nodded, a little disdainful, perhaps, and she raised her near-empty flute in a not-quite-reciprocal gesture of good will. Clearly she had worked out her own way of dealing with his present situation, and she didn't wish to deviate from her chosen course. But there was something in that woman's look—proud, threatening, and beneath that, he had imagined, a little terrified, too, that had reminded Mr. Stiers now of the look on his daughter's face when he had confronted her the very last time. The particulars didn't seem to matter now, not since she had fled and all but disappeared from the earth. Actually, it had to do with some drugs he had discovered, quite by accident, among her belongings, when he was searching for a book of his in the apartment so many years ago.

That last altercation had proven fatal to his relationship with his daughter. It had turned, quite unexpectedly, ugly, and looking back on it now, as Mr. Stiers bit carefully into his salad before him of arugula and cheese, he wondered if anything in the world were so simple after all. He wondered whether that woman on New Year's Eve had ever found herself really happy. He hoped she had. Perhaps she already was, even that night. Moreover, Mr. Stiers wondered what his daughter was doing, and whether she was in the city after all.

Resolved, he promised himself he would make his visit, deciding finally that his life was a shortening proposition and that it was his role to search her out and to find out if she were okay. It was as simple as that. He regretted now that he hadn't called and invited Felice and her partner along to dinner even now. It didn't bother him that there in the restaurant, seated by himself, he might appear, to an impartial observer anyway, to a be a little lost, a little dried-up, a little cut off from the noise and bustle of people and the current of feeling that he knew to be the substance of life.

***

The next morning, his cabby, in person, spoke without a Cockney accent. Instead, he was from Pakistan, which Mr. Stiers took to be a good sign right away.

"Where to then?" the cabby asked. His name was Francis, from his license, which was displayed curiously upside-down on the dashboard of the cab.

Mr. Stiers gave the address by rote, a little putoff perhaps. He distrusted cab rides as a rule and didn't like the fact that he didn't know exactly where he was going. He didn't want to be taken advantage of, not in his present situation anyway, not when he was mulling over what he might say to Felice in his head if he indeed did find her at home. It was twelve o'clock. She would have to be up, of course, but he didn't know whether she would be at work, even on a Saturday.

After he gave the address and the cab started to move, Mr. Stiers pretended to be involved in looking where they were headed. The destination was in Kensington, actually. There he was, being driven through the dreary air on a fall day in London, trying his best not to be taken advantage of yet readying himself to say anything to have his daughter understand him after all. It was strange and a little frightening all at once, he thought now.

The driver got them there in just over a halfhour. He turned his tiny car into a boulevard lined with a few trees. It was evidently a modest neighborhood, Mr. Stiers noticed, but he saw that as the cabby and he watched the numbers count upward toward the correct address, the section of buildings where Felice lived was actually quite posh, a townhouse in fact, and the driver seemed to indicate as much as he accepted Mr. Stiers' fare and small gratuity.

"Going to visit royalty?" the man named Francis proffered, quite good-naturedly.

Mr. Stiers was put a bit off-balance by this but recovered quickly, like a child's toy spinning on the floor righting itself, though still wobbling, when carelessly knocked off its axis.

"It's my daughter's place, "Mr. Stiers replied. "She's expecting me, if you must know," he added, as he climbed out of the cab. Before he shut the door behind him, the driver asked if he should wait for his customer to conduct his business or at least to see if he found his way into the building.

"No thank you," Mr. Stiers said as the taxi sped off. Naturally, he wanted to take another cab back to his hotel when it was over. Because he had no idea what would happen with Felice; he had no idea how long it would take.

He approached the townhouse, which appeared to have a small courtyard at its side. The place was surrounded by an iron fence, which was not locked, he found, and he walked through the gate and up the steps to the door. He checked for names on the outside of the door, but there were none. So, he started at the topmost button and pressed it gently, as if sounding an alarm somewhere.

A woman's voice came over the speaker, but it was so garbled he couldn't make out what it said exactly, much less whether its timbre matched that of his daughter.

He tried a second button: once, twice, and a third time, with increasing confidence as it became clear there was no one home.

Then he collected himself and pressed the third button—there were only four, and he was running out of chances now. *Why was it always the third button?* he thought out loud, talking to himself, and pressing and waiting.

He felt a drop of rain now on his face and worried that it might rain on him after all, though the sky remained ordinary and dreary and didn't seem to threaten with anything immediate.

"Who is it?" another woman's voice said. It was clearly not his daughter's voice. It was older and noticeably accented English.

"Felice?" he said anyway, excited. His heart was very much in his throat now. And Mr. Stiers found it was not an unpleasant feeling.

"Come on up," the voice continued, "You're expected," it said, quite implausibly. But Mr. Stiers obeyed anyhow.

The lock on the door buzzed and withdrew its bolt from the doorframe. The heavy door opened quite easily at his bewildered touch. He walked up two flights of stairs to the third floor, where the voice logically must have resided, taking the last two steps in one bound. He walked over the clear carpeted hallway and toward the door.

He knocked politely, and the same voice returned with its original question.

"Who is it, then?" it asked.

Before he could explain, the door opened to reveal a fifty-ish woman wearing a floral print dress with a ruffled white collar.

"You're not the plumber, I suspect," she commented at once, brightly. Her face was ebullient, nonetheless. She looked as though she didn't get much company and didn't mind his intrusion.

She explained that her sink had been clotted with tea leaves, of all things, and she had summoned a plumber the very first thing in the morning.

"No, of course not," he replied to her question. "My name is Stiers, Ryan Stiers." He was getting used to explaining himself.

He explained that his daughter Felice may have changed her last name by now, but that he nonetheless believed she lived in this very building.

"She lives downstairs," the woman said, "But they haven't been there the past few weeks, I'd say."

The woman's name was Edith Ganders. She invited Mr. Stiers in, and he acceded only after she said she was on good terms with his daughter. She led him with her small uncomfortable steps to a spacious sitting room, which was nearly spartan. There was a monolithic blue settee, upon which Mr. Stiers sat carefully, not knowing what to expect.

As if by magic, Mrs. Ganders appeared with some tea.

"I'm sure Felice speaks very highly of you," Mrs. Ganders said to him.

"I don't think so," Mr. Stiers said. He explained, without going into more detail than was necessary, that he and his daughter had their difficulties, but he knew that they would outlast them all. "Grudges have no place," Mr. Stiers said. "It's all too short," he went on.

"It must be difficult to have children nowadays," Mrs. Ganders commiserated. She explained that she and her husband were childless.

She sipped her tea and looked at a stranger, out the window and onto the courtyard. She looked to be a woman of understanding herself, and Mr. Stiers was certain with Mrs. Ganders on his side, Felice would hear him out. Things would be well, he thought.

After Mrs. Ganders promised to hand-deliver the letter from Mr. Stiers to his daughter, he gave her his business card too, as well as precise instructions for Felice to contact him. He turned, quite cheered now, and departed. He walked by what he took to be Felice's apartment, whose door was no different, he found, than any of the other doors in the building.

Back on the street, it was drizzling unavoidably now, and so Mr. Stiers unfolded his umbrella, with its carved wooden shaft and knobbed handle. He resolved that he would remain quite dry. He took the three or four steps down to the iron gate and frowned when he saw that it had been left ajar. He opened it to allow his safe passage and then closed the latch back to its proper position.

He found that despite the rain he wasn't nearly annoyed with things as they stood, though he would no doubt have trouble finding a cab in this part of the city. He looked both ways on the street, knowing he would have to walk up toward the main boulevard to find a taxi.

From the back, she could have been anyone. She was small, she wore flat-soled shoes and a gray raincoat. It was her umbrella he recognized, a dull red parasol, which she still possessed incongruously after all these years. She walked slowly up ahead, and before he could even begin thinking about it, before his head caught up with his old man's heart, he was almost running up the street to catch up with her, not even wondering what he would say first to Felice, who as if sensing the length of his journey, at the very last moment, turned to face her smiling father.

The Dangerous Pigeons
of San Marco

They were arguing in Venice, right across the bright-blue, hazy waters in front of the former hotel of Henry James. The guidebook said you could make out the salt-washed façade of the writer's old pensione over the water, looking over from the landing in front of San Giorgio. Water lapped in the heat as she exploded in anger, for no reason, letting him know how she felt. He stood in the closed air of the vaporetto, shell-shocked. She was in her sunhat and dark sunglasses. He couldn't see her eyes. The vaporetto docked, jostled once or twice, and stopped. They got off quickly. He watched her move to the waiting stand with its glass and its pillars.

They all came to Venice to die, Chopin, Wagner, Pound, who else? she thought. This thick air did no one any good, though the sea promised much. It was a city for lovers, for art, music, for harlequin mimes. The mask with the long beak formed a repetitive figure as they strolled along the narrow walkways of the city. The plague doctor who came to your room in the last hours. The city seemed unreal. It was so hot, and the sun was too bright.

***

She was angry at him for choosing the wrong vaporetto but in equal measure upset with herself for being that kind of person. "I am not nice," she once said. She possessed an impatient soul, a secret reserve of wanderlust, a stone-hearted resolve, too, prevalent two or three generations back in her mother's line. Venice was so hot in late July, and her poor lummox of a boyfriend was complaining too much, too fat, too sweaty, too American. From the first day, he'd been getting in her way during their tour.

They had dated back in New York for about a year before the opportunity of a lifetime to work in Italy had surfaced. She had moved six months before his arrival, and she felt she had been transformed. Part of her thought the boy might fall in love with Italy too, but from the very start, it didn't seem like he fit in.

He sweated and complained when they climbed the Duomo back in Florence, as they scaled the hill in the Boboli Gardens to have a granita in the welcome shade of the polyglot refreshment stand where she heard half a dozen languages spoken at adjacent tables. She could put up with him then, but not now, not in this drastic Venetian heat and sun, which seemed to draw every bit of moisture out of the lapping Adriatic. And the vaporetti were pressure cookers of humidity, greenhouses of discontent. All this beauty drifting by the window as the boat made its way up the Grand Canal. It moved from side to side, of course, to permit the tourists to cross the waters by boat instead of on foot at the improvised wooden Accademia Bridge or by gondola. They had guessed wrong with the previous vaporetto and were deposited on the steps of the church across from Giudecca, far away from their hotel.

The water licking the plain marble landing, the church's simple marble façade was a pocket of heat, too, at midday.

She was mad at him and herself for hating him at this moment, for being frustrated with his complaints, his lack of sprezzatura. He made traveling look so difficult, so impossible. She wanted to give him a big slap against his sun-reddened face shiny with sweat and too much sunscreen. He was so weak, so petulant. He was taking her spirit down with his. How could he complain when it was so glorious, all of it, the heat, the light, the sculpture, the uncanny layout of that glorious labyrinth of streets that made up the small, brilliant city? How could he ruin it for her like this, though he had been romantic too, kissing her in the restaurant last night after a truly delicious dinner, the twice-fermented Amarone. He had his good points too, and he was good with directions. He was never lost in the city. He was like a big fat pigeon, overgrown like one of the thousands or millions in St. Mark's Square. Or he was some kind of super-intelligent St. Bernard, nosing his way around the place. Especially at twilight or at night, her boy could walk quickly. She liked following him around in the darkness, hopping over a foot bridge, every turn presenting a new view of the city, exposing some scenic corner, the smell of the canal, usually fetid unexpectedly but sometimes a fresh breeze. He was sure-footed with his little foldable tourist map. He had a remarkable sense of direction. He got them to dinner in ten minutes, and they were five minutes early at the secret cafe for their prenotazione.

But this was all lost to her now. She saw Tintoretto's red, glaring with an old-world look of revenge and heartlessness, the look given before the last twist of the knife perhaps, when the victim was already mortally injured. What part of her enjoyed the poor boy's suffering?. Lost, alone, and hopelessly overheated. They waited in silence for the next boat coming from the opposite direction over the waters across from the Lido. This boat was packed with dozens of sunbathers, real Italians smelling of sand and too much sun and sweat and seawater. They were gloriously at ease with their red faces, garrulous, joyous at being able to experience the Lido on such a gorgeous Sunday like this. While she and the boy both glowered, not looking at each other, standing carefully amidst the young and old bodies of the sun-fed Italians, hoping that the wind would shift a little and give a rift to that invisible curtain of heat that engulfed them all there, though the Italians would never seem to notice. They gloried in it, all this sunlight. It was theirs. But her boy suffered greatly, she could see the pained look on his puffy-eyed, red face. That dumbfounded American face that demanded quite stupidly that the whole world conform to his standards. *How could there be heat like this?* he was thinking. Even if he loved Venice in his own way—at dinner he was effusive, and on a normal day of touring he became quite the talker, reading the tourist guide and stupidly pointing out what was what as if she didn't know twice as much as he did. Well, she let him have his little moments like this when he thought he was superior. She liked it when he took an interest in things, especially this beautiful city. "Venice," he said, "was a thinking man's Disneyland." That was stolen from someone famous, of course, she didn't know exactly, but his other line was better. "Venice is a perfect architectural model of itself, drawn to a one-to-one scale," he said.

***

Back in the airconditioned hotel, they slept off their anger. They took cooling showers separately, and the anger left their bodies along with the heat. The combined effect of jet lag and near heatstroke and frustration with each other gave way to the deepest sleep. She let go of the world completely, sleeping for ten or twelve hours, a Snow White of Venice, deep in REM, dreaming of the city, getting lost and found. In the dream, the city was so much cooler, the exact temperature of the hotel room it seemed. She was looking for him and he was lost to her. She was standing on a bridge surrounded by a remarkable emptiness on all sides of her. It was strange how in the crowded city, even with thousands of smiling tourists, one could take a turn or two and find oneself utterly and completely alone, as if the last person on earth. The effect was magical and was soon broken by a horde of European teenagers with their inevitable backpacks, or a lost-looking American family, mother, father, and son and daughter in tow, a look of profound disorientation on all four lost American faces.

But for a few moments anyway, Venice doled out its small epiphanies. In the dream, she was looking in all four directions, and she was alone. She had absolutely no idea where she was. The thought was oddly comforting. She called out his name, feeling responsible somehow. Perhaps it was her fault that he had gone off with his map, charging ahead like an explorer in his blind confidence. But he had just kept going, never looking back for her, and she let him run off ahead into the labyrinth. Who knows what mythical creature lay waiting and wishing him harm? Venice was safe enough, especially at midday like this, and he was gone into its farthest corner. Perhaps he would realize his mistake and turn around and notice that she was no longer following. Or he would just keep navigating his way through the maze, ending up in the sea, into the warm green summer Adriatic.

She called out his name once more though it was hopeless. The dream had run its course like a play. She awoke breathing with absolute calm in long, regular breaths. His fat stupid head was turned away from her. He was probably drooling on the pillow. He was snoring a little. Yet she loved him then completely, with a silly, reckless abandon. He was stupid and garrulous and snoring away like a family pet. He was a work in progress, she knew that, and she hated him for it at times. But he never got lost. He knew right away where he was in any kind of weather, in any city, really. And though he tired easily in the heat of the journey and misbehaved quite often, he knew where he was going, and she admired that a little. He wasn't so bad after all. They were a good pair, the two of them. She knew more than he did, but let him navigate here in the city, even if she knew her way around on her own, of course. If only they didn't get angry with one another, like that afternoon. She regretted it now and kissed him awake. He chortled and made impossible dog-like sounds. He woke up smiling, sunburnt, and alive to her. She had never felt so rested herself.

***

Their adventure had begun in Florence, where she had taken a job with a college teaching French to American students. It was the first week of the boy's visit, and they had planned the weekend in Venice.

On the second day he had come out of the bathroom, dripping wet, covered only in a towel, bleeding.

"I think I've hurt myself," he said. She wondered what on earth now. "My head," he said, sitting on her chair. He was leaving little droplets of pink water everywhere on the perfect Italian floor. She resisted the urge to clean those up before attending to their source.

"Your mirror attacked me," he said.

He had a nasty gash on his head. She examined the injury right on the top of his cranium, just where the part was.

"It doesn't look too bad," she said. In fact, it looked pretty awful. She was mothering him now a little. The first time alone in her perfectly clean and newly redecorated apartment, and her clumsy boy did this.

He couldn't see at all without his contacts, as blind as one of those clumsy birds in Piazza di Independenza, she thought.

She made him an improvised ice pack with a paper towel and some ice cubes. She tried to calm him down; her ridiculous boy shivering from fear and panic, still wet. He was a child again, and she couldn't respect him now, not like that.

They had a train to Venice to catch in two hours. She wanted to take him to the hospital instead.

"I'm not going to the hospital," he said. "Who knows where I'll wind up there?"

Instead, they fashioned a butterfly stitch out of a bandage. She trimmed the hair around the wound as he winced in pain. The cut wasn't deep, a triangular flap of skin carved out by her ancient mirror, which swung out over him as he bent over to throw out a disposable shaving blade. He'd missed, he said, and wanting to be a good houseguest, bent down to pick up the blade. When he did, the mirror swung out and his head impacted its heavy leaden edge directly on the top of his head with the full force of a quick upthrust of his legs. He saw stars and then touched the wound, shocked at the amount blood on his fingers.

Later, they bought bandages in the Stazione Michelangelo, waiting in line with other tourists as advice and remedies were dispensed by an old apothecary with noticeably bad teeth. There was a woman with a bad sunburn, a tall backpacker with a cracked tooth, an old Florentine woman filling a prescription, all moving at an unbelievably slow, Italianate pace. The boy was still wounded and perhaps in shock, too exhausted to fight back, not pouting or complaining in his typical American fashion. She bought him a set of bandages and some topical antiseptic for her ministrations later in the Venetian hotel room.

To conceal his injury, he wore a hat on the train like a baseball fan or worse, stock-car racing fan. She was secretly aghast. He was embarrassingly American and looked so lost between the fat Italian grandma and her two granddaughters who were traveling to Padua in the same train car.

Still, she worried the boy might have a concussion or something, and she wanted to wake him up as he dozed in and out of consciousness in the way of all jet-lagged travelers catching up on their sleep while in motion. The train moved gracefully over green Tuscan fields and the occasional tunnel which closed the outside world off to its passengers. They were suddenly uncomfortably close in the bright light of the car. She tried not to look at him. They had reserved seats that were placed directly across from one another, but she couldn't help noticing his reflection in the window opposite, doubly reflected in a trick of optics, doubled surfaces, as if to torment her even when she was trying not to look at him. The wounded boy and his unfortunate hat hiding his damaged head.

On the first day of their visit in Venice, on a Saturday, she found a grocery store tucked into the back of a building in Canareggio, next to a footbridge. She had settled in, clearly, and was secretly proud of the fact that she was able to find a grocery store in a city teeming with tourists. The boy pouted. He was too big, too awkward to navigate successfully between the narrow, crowded aisles packed with the usual Italian delicacies and basic foodstuffs. That's how they bought the raw materials for their picnic. The boy paid, generously enough, but he was a dolt when it came to the money system and the way it was done, and he had forgotten to weigh the apples in the produce section, the way they did it there, and he had no clue as to what the cashier was yelling at him for, of course. He didn't fit in, though he could learn, and she knew she had no reason to demand that he know such things. He was just a guest, a foreign interloper, a tourist, and she was settling in, or trying hard to.

She was becoming an Italian. She would have to choose.

She took the bag of apples herself and apologized to the checkout woman, who was perhaps fifty, heavyset, and histrionically angry at her wounded American tourist still donning the ugly baseball cap.

"Mi dispiace," she said. She spoke carefully in her best accent, trying to sound local and authentic. The befuddled boy looked around for a

sympathetic soul, not finding one, as the store was clearly meant for the
real Venetians, who probably felt guilty enough that they weren't going
to the shops or the outdoor markets for individual meats, seafood,
produce, breads, and desserts, but it was so convenient, this new place,
at least without this tourist here. Who told this outsider, this foreigner,
that this place was here anyway?

That night, they didn't hold one another. They only kissed
goodnight. He even slept clumsily, she thought. She dreamt he was
a large bird which came into her apartment back in Florence. He had
an oily green hood and he was immensely round, clucking, running
into and knocking over things in her tidy apartment. In the dream,
the bird boy, this pigeon, came out of the bathroom with a bleeding
head, grotesque in the way of nightmares, missing an eye, though the
subconscious camera didn't dwell on that. He was memberless, she
noticed, there was nothing between the pigeon's legs that she could
find. Just a ruff of dirty matted feathers, her eunuch pigeon boy.

He was about to peck her when she woke up. His foot was bothering
her, and he had stolen the sheet, which, though it was madly hot outside,
was actually a comfort in the aria condizione of the hotel room.

Of course, now that she was acclimated to the climate, she had
no use for air conditioning, like the real Italians, and she was actually
shivering, unpleasantly cold. He even slept selfishly, she noticed. She
pushed him away a bit, carefully, and went back to sleep, a dream-
less, perfect, solitary slumber till the Venetian sun woke both of them
through the shutter backed up by the perfect blue of an Adriatic sky
and the muffled chime of the campanile, which was just over from
the palazzo-turned-hotel, one of the many local parish churches in
a Venice still divided by old neighborhoods loyal to one church, a
patchwork of ringing bells, she imagined, everyone growing up with a
familiar timbre of hours struck in a familiar voice which signaled home
to anyone who belonged here.

For the first time, she was conscious of her tourist-ness in Venice.
She belonged in Firenze, that's where she belonged. She was once an
outsider, and so was the boy, of course, who could only appreciate and
walk around with an aesthetic appetite (she supposed) for the sights
and old buildings that came upon one shimmering off the water even

more beautifully and unexpectedly than one of those watercolors by Sargent, who she knew always got Venice exactly right in its extraordinary tentativeness of the moment in the right trick of water and light. You couldn't conquer Venice, you couldn't say you had seen it all, never, for around the corner, it was always new. There was always a new building, a new epiphany, a coupling of water and sunlight and architectural detail that was never in the guidebooks. No, her boy might want to see every major point of interest in their three days (though to his credit he loved sitting in the Giardinni writing postcards back home, perhaps making sketches of the sea, or having a picnic). The best of Venice was in her quiet corners, the modest canal (not the great one), the ordinary neighborhood footbridge, an unexpected ordinary building that was, the guidebook might say for instance, the childhood home of Marco Polo, just one example, or a church that was locked down most of the time but housed an unexpected treasure of Carpaccio's telling the story of St. George and the Dragon, which she knew was important for whatever reason for the Venetians. All these modest moments would be lost on the boy, who strutted through the various tiny streets as if a Nineteenth Century explorer on a mission to put a flag in the next discovery, getting from point A to point B as quickly and efficiently as possible. She let him lead her when they were in a hurry, making it to a restaurant in time for their prenotazione, but if they had some time, she would drive him crazy, she suspected, with her improvised perambulations here and there, finding Ruskin's house or where Milton stood or where Wagner stayed in his last days. Her boy was interested enough, or pretended to be. The city was its own map of embedded history. To an extent, it was alright to play at being tourist here, Venice was in the middle of things, just as St. Mark's Place was the center of a cacophony of visitors from all over the world placed in close proximity to one another. In the famous piazza, the people were as plentiful as those clucking permanent residents, the pigeons, which were the one fully constant in the city's history, perhaps, along with the water and Adriatic sun.

She was surrounded by pigeons. St. Mark's was glorious, but those ruffling rats, airborne vermin in the piazza, thronging in multiples of the tourists from every land. She was perhaps the only one who found them abominable. No, she couldn't have been the only one. They were a filthy gray and flew in dirty packs, like innumerable vermin, roosting in every nook and crevice of the nearby Museo Ducale, whose architectural details seemed to have thousands of nesting places on every nook and cranny of stone.

The boy held both hands outstretched with a piece of bread from lunch. Pigeons alighted on him, three, four, five, and he was laughing as they nibbled out of both hands. He forced her to take a picture, and she did, but she found the camera just wouldn't hold still and the image was blurred.

Later, whenever she thought of the usual glories of Venezia, her thoughts were always seized, crowded out by images of the horrible feral birds. There was even a poster advertising action by the city to contain the wild, dangerous, feral pigeons. It was a campaign to drum up support for a bit of culling, though the poster was clear, as far as she could tell in her still improving Italian, that this would not affect those who raised pigeons on their own. The puffed up image selected for the poster was of an oily-green-breasted male, at least a two-foot high on the poster with bold type surrounding his head. He looked dangerous enough, so full of himself, so needlessly proud, as if it was the pigeons who owned the old beautiful palazzi, and the unfed glowing canals, not the Venetians themselves.

***

Back in Florence, on the last day of the boy's visit, they went to the movies near the historical district, an American gangster picture dubbed in Italian. The boy squirmed and fidgeted. He couldn't follow the dialogue very well, but he was a good sport. They didn't hold hands in the theater anymore. They were friendly though, and even shared some chocolate as the film rolled on.

It had rained while they were inside, and as they came out onto the piazza, a few blocks away from the Duomo, which could be seen rising over the building adjacent to the square, she noticed the pearly mists over the cobblestones. She felt this was somehow the spirit of the old city, and it was hers alone. She didn't say anything to the boy. She knew she had chosen this place now, and the boy didn't fit into the tableau. It wasn't his fault, it was just the way things stood.

***

She rode in the taxi to the airport the next morning. She waited with him in the terminal, and they said goodbye. They had espresso and pastries from the takeaway stand. They kissed goodbye, and he got on his plane, a twin-engine turboprop with a round gray belly. It didn't look like it could fly at all, oblong and somehow less than aerodynamic as it stood on the ground.

On the runway, she imagined the boy might be waving. He was a sentimentalist after all.

The mountains were high around the airport. The plane had to do all it could to get enough altitude to clear the peaks. After twenty minutes of waiting on the tarmac, she watched the plane smooth its way down the runway and take to the skies. It made a steep ascent, and it was only by a trick of perspective that she imagined it might have been going too low. For a terrible instant she thought she saw a puff of smoke. Perhaps the nonchalant Italians in the airport would run to the windows to get a glimpse of a tragedy.

She watched the awkward little turbojet climb into the misty Italian morning, now airborne, now as graceful as a grey little bird. He would never be coming back, of course. It was just that way. She made sure he was safe over the mountains that surrounded the old city and ringed in the smog of a thousand Vespas. She felt lighter and freer already as she turned to go back to her brand-new life.

The Trouble with Fire

That was about the time we angels went missing. We forgot all about your children's theology, of guarding anyone from danger or temptation or madness or a slippery first step that would lead to a life of crime and dissipation. Naturally enough, we are conscious, invisible beings. We don't have physical forms, though with special dispensation from the Higher Ups—well, you have to know the right people, and let's face it, divine providence bumps along pretty slowly nowadays—we can briefly take a physical shape. Forget all those Renaissance triptychs with Gabriel and the Annunciation or Michael helping St. George slay a dragon or some other mythical beast. That sappy black-and-white movie from 1939 got most of it right. We can take a form for a day or two, but always to solve a crucial challenge, a man doubting everything at Christmas about to jump off a bridge, that sort of thing. A few years after the lovely German movie about the angels, well, my favorite one, actually, a bureaucrat made a phone call to bring down the Iron Curtain.

You'd like to think he overheard the thoughts of his better angels. Don't skimp on human effort. That's pretty important, too, for getting things done. But I'm a realist, and there are those who are lot less practically minded. How is the Berlin Wall like a veil? Discuss.

Things went wrong in other ways, too. We don't have much of an appreciation of time, which is remarkably fluid for anyone. If you've ever taken a train or a plane, of course, you already know that. There are the inevitable difficulties of perceiving time and its limits after eons spent watching and appreciating human affairs at such a great distance. But the most relevant fact in all this is the sense of relief, of something happening in real time.

Watching from On High for All Eternity is godawful boring. Did you ever watch evolutionary selection? That reluctant bearded Victorian dashed all the old biblical versions of time, and extended it into the millions and billions of years. Well, under the old system, let me tell you, things moved a good deal faster. Creating the Universe in six days. Well, that was something to watch. Even the Genesis storyteller doesn't point out how marvelous this was to us (well, we weren't always around, but you probably suspected that). The Earth from the chaotic Void, light from darkness, land from the waters, and life in all its bewildering complexity. Then comes Darwin and its billions of years of the smallest change, brown feathers, not white ones, heavier beaks, sharper eyes. Yada, yada, yada. Have you ever watched plankton evolve? Not something to write home about.

Your invention of art was a big surprise to us. A few scribbles with charcoal on the side of a cave. The observing angel in charge of that one didn't know what to make of it. Were you telling a story of your latest kill? Wishing for more meat to be sent from the void? Some of us thought so. Or just passing time beautifully like us, your observers, who were so often bored? We had a meeting with the Higher Ups about that one. We weren't sure you were up to any good with it, that thing with drawing pictures. Early on, we didn't think much of it. After all, you couldn't do your scratchings all day. It was impossible. You still had to hunt and gather and all that in order to survive. It was only thousands of years later when you started to have a few of you do this sort of thing twenty-four-seven. That became a problem, as we soon figured out. The moral dissipation of the artist. No one saw that one coming either. It was a bad idea from the start. But it began wonderfully enough: writing on the walls like a child and that weird fascinated look the first scribblers had in the darkness and filth of your early abodes.

Much later, books were met with initial suspicion, too, but soon we saw that they moved slowly enough that we could still keep track of you. Watching the first man and woman reading to their child, now that was a beautiful memory for us. Even the most adept scholar or philosopher moved pretty slowly. We read over your shoulder and heard you thinking your slow Latinate thoughts in between the printed words. In fact, books were the perfect medium for us. They deepened the sense of who you were. We almost grew to love you.

The trouble started much later. It was Prometheus again, all that fuss with fire. We didn't see it at first (wrong church, after all, the Greeks and their denizens of Olympus and all that—we didn't talk as much as we should have). We left well enough alone but should have seen the trouble coming.

I think the problem with your kind began with the wireless radio. All those voices transmitted into the void, moving over the land and sky at the uniform speed of light. Imagine all those thoughts that much be tracked by our cadre of observers. Radio did it first, and of course the telephone, then television, now your computer networks and all the words and images and noise that interfere with any sense of order at all.

When you started watching tiny screens, you became a lot like us. At first, we were envious.

Now, we travel pretty well and fast enough, but even we can't dart back and forth as quickly as you can nowadays. Of course, you used your new capabilities in all sorts of unpredictable ways. And that's where more trouble started. All those diverse thoughts generated by random messages and images. It was bewildering to us, and a little sad. We didn't want you to use your gifts like that.

Monitoring your communications was just plain exhausting (and the thoughts that went with them). I forget whether we went AWOL first or just stop listening. We couldn't tell if you were studying philosophy or the latest Hollywood gossip. We didn't care, and you predictably made things worse. Some of us did the old trick of asking to see one virtuous man or woman in the whole of creation. It was almost a rhetorical question by now. This one used to be easy, because there was always some serious-minded man or woman far from the beaten path. But it didn't matter. The Higher Ups had done away with that sort of thing two thousand years ago, anyway. New regime and all that. Gentler sense of crime and punishment. Revised penal code. We liked it, too. Easier for us when most offenses weren't permanent and capital. A lot less responsibility for us. It made our jobs a good deal more enjoyable. Rather like your naturalists of old watching the behavior of finches. We watched and took copious notes but never once judged.

Of course, who wants to track the velleities of city dwellers on their mobile phones? The realization among the practical ones: angels like us became a sort of state apparatus, the kind of baddies in your history books who were looking into everything about their people, where they went, what they had for lunch, their phone calls tapped and transcribed in increasingly arcane detail. Everyone had a dossier back then in the terrestrial sphere. And for us, though we certainly didn't do any paperwork, there was a sense of keeping records, an angel's eidetic memory, after all, was exhaustive and permanent. But where were the bright overheard thoughts of earlier times, the silent, serious thinking among crowds that we used to cherish so deeply? Where did that go? Had your new sort of fire extinguished this sort of thing? Would it ever come back? And was it inevitable to have gone so wrong like that? Honestly, we were starting to wonder.

Metronome

In the summer of his twenty-sixth year (he was twenty-five, actually, but preferred to remember that by the time anyone counted a year, it would already be extinguished), he gave up the world and retired from his life in the cities, where he had gone to school and worked at a variety of positions, back to his parents' home in the flatlands. He took a job typing at a real estate agency. He read books about exiles. He read about Wittgenstein moving to a small village and talking to no one except its parson. He read about Glenn Gould, who left the concert stage for the hermit's world of the recording studio, on an old record jacket with the photograph of the tormented master dressed in black in the corner of an empty studio, his long limbs draped over a chair, in every regard the picture of the difficult genius. And he read about doddering Beethoven, deaf and recalcitrant in his last days. He bought a blank book of music staves, intent on composing his first work. Mostly, he went to his job, came home, and played his music as if it were a kind of purification. Though he usually enjoyed solitude, there was no denying Kristoph felt a little lost, and the people he read about were no help to him either.

The only thing that Kristoph required of himself and others was complete honesty. That was perhaps one reason that he found himself at this stage in his life almost completely alone. He found that his parents were honest people; his mother was a schoolteacher and his father was an electrician, both getting ready for retirement. They never minced words, nor were they particularly diplomatic. Growing up, they said what they felt needed to be said. Only now were the creeping half-lies and the shades of truth getting mixed into everything they said, too.

Like all parents, they wanted him to do something more. What that was, they weren't sure. Some part of him, the part that couldn't resist overhearing his mother's voice on the phone, her evasions regarding his present situation when speaking with other relatives, half suspected he was fast becoming a family secret.

"You have nothing to be ashamed of," his mother said, gray and tired looking, though he didn't believe that she meant it really. He paid them for room and board anyway, though they protested, of course, to keep himself honest. He hated freeloading, and that was probably one reason his life in the cities had never worked out for him. Kristoph couldn't accept the logic of networking, that to find a job and an apartment seemed a matter of word-of-mouth, a conspiracy of friendship. Since he didn't have that many friends, he never really seemed to fit into the city.

His father liked having him around the house again, though he worried about his son's long-term prospects. They talked sometimes about starting a small business together.

Kristoph's older brother Rudy called from Chicago, where he now lived, to give him advice.

"I want to help you," Rudy said. "You should be out there."

The vague sense of this phrase plagued Kristoph: it meant perhaps finding a job with more of a future, or perhaps dating someone seriously, or just going out more with friends. Meanwhile, Kristoph began to avoid talking to his brother on the phone.

He suspected he made his parents feel a little younger. Yet they made him feel like an ineffectual ghost, one that could look over the scenes of his youth but who could have nothing to do with it anymore. Moreover, almost everyone he had grown up with had moved on too, and so it was easy to pretend that he had no past at all.

Mostly, until he figured things out, Kristoph decided to keep to himself.

He had been playing music for twenty years or so. Yet he had never performed for anyone—except himself. Like in most things in his life, he carried high standards, and sometimes he would pretend that he was onstage somewhere. But except for these moments of silent imagination, he was otherwise unassuming in every respect. He was outwardly modest and reserved.

If he got home early from work, he could play his parents' upright piano, but what he really lived for was to drive into town and sneak into the conservatory, which was about fifteen minutes away. There, they seldom checked I.D.s—and he looked like a connie—a music student. He had the short-cropped hair, the requisite black overcoat. He was always dressed quite impeccably despite his finances, which were in shambles. He might have been a piano major. His hands were large enough, long fingers, slightly bony knuckles. He had no trouble at all playing tenths across the keyboard.

One day, he walked through the lobby of the place with all its chattering, nerve-wracked gossip.

"I heard Katrina cried in studio today," someone said.

"I hate him, he has perfect pitch, the bastard."

And a comment through a clenched grin, "I really loved your recital." The attitude behind it ineffable: envious, admiring, or homicidal, Kristoph couldn't begin to guess. These people were generally too complicated, he suspected, for their own good.

Often, he waited to use the phone in the lobby of the conservatory, where he marveled at the odd species of genius that flourished all around that room. They reminded him of vampires, the pale skin, the nervous, bloodless complexions. They chain-smoked, heavy, unfiltered cigarettes, which made him cough—he was slightly allergic to smoke.

Yet he would have, at another time in his life perhaps, given anything to join them.

Then Kristoph walked down the narrow corridors, listening half in wonder, half nervously, keeping an eye out for the student who worked as a monitor in the place. Inevitably it was a militant type, a boy in a kelly-green turtleneck sweater and a book on Wagner or something. Usually, during daylight hours, there was nobody posted at all. If there were, Kristoph would just walk outside around the doors of the practice room complex—there were close to two hundred cubicles in all spread out on two floors, most with a baby grand stationed in each—and wait. He pretended to read until someone emerged from the building, and then he walked into the place on his own.

Today, though, this was unnecessary, and Kristoph walked through the conservatory lobby, past the recording studio where he heard trumpets and drums and electric bass, and then past the pipe organs, which thrummed all the way down the hall. He walked past a dozen or so practice rooms. In all, three or four violinists rocked back and forth, their bows slicing the air, each playing in some impossibly intricate passage, like beautiful, noisy insects bottled up behind their doors. The rooms were not entirely soundproof, and there were so many of them. On busy days, Kristoph could wander around for ten minutes, searching for an empty one, and the effect was as though a dozen radios were left on together, the sounds from each chamber colliding. Individually in each room, every sound, every nuance was so calculated, but when run together, heard from the outside, the effect was a complicated, uneven noise that made him a bit nervous, it was so out-of-control. And he was not someone to get nervous easily.

On his way to a back room that he was fond of, hopefully away from everyone who might be listening in, Kristoph passed four or five rooms charged with the sound of the Steinways and the manic gesticulations of their players, which he glimpsed through the narrow windows. As always, someone was playing Rachmaninoff from memory for their senior concerto competition, performing on a level that he really couldn't comprehend.

His own playing was a bit too analytical, he suspected. He broke a classical piece down into smaller bits and traced each voice where it began, following it like a fish leaping and diving across a body of water until it emerged on the other side of the lake. He played things slowly and build up speed like a distance runner learning to run sprints. But it was never fast enough. He had to think about it, his hands' every move, and the music always resisted that kind of calculation.

These people behind the glass did things differently. It just came to them, their music. They just looked at the score and knew. The hands just followed something deep down in the brain. The thought came later, if at all. No one asked why they could pound the keys like a banshee at six years of age and produce real music, it just happened, and one didn't even think to be thankful for it.

At first Kristoph had been envious, he admitted it, but a while later he found he just didn't worry about it. It was still what he loved, sitting behind a Steinway in one of these rooms and forgetting entirely about how many notes there were.

He wasn't in competition with anyone, not really, because he played jazz, standards mostly—Porter, Gershwin, Kern, and most of this he was free to make up himself. This was a kind of freedom. He stayed away from heavy, chromatic turf. He just let each voice sing the way it wanted. That's what it was. His teacher always said that he had a great left hand. He just let it go where it wanted, on its own rhythm, comping to God Bless the Child or something, and he was happy.

Kristoph wondered sometimes, when someone walked by, whether they thought he was really one of them. He suspected that they didn't, that they just shook their heads and reassured themselves that he was nothing to worry about for senior competition, that he was no ace-in-the-hole, the unremarkable sophomore who suddenly in his senior year came out like a battleship with Liszt's Totentanz, all crescendo and bombast and rippling ninths and tenths all over the ivories. And after that sudden victory, who knew? Other competitions, concert appearances, and maybe even a few recordings, at least a master's degree at Juilliard. He knew they had nothing to worry about from him, however. He was self-occupied and content with his loose improvisations upon a theme, with his borrowed baby grand piano, its finish pockmarked from the endless repetition of scales from a hundred diligent connies (the "S" in Steinway had been eaten away, in fact, by their collective rigor). He himself had no use for scales and exercises, which he always did, grudgingly, if at all.

So, Kristoph played on his own, in private, stealing some time from the world for his music.

But today, an hour into his practice session, the monitor came and knocked at his door to ask him to leave. Kristoph explained that he had forgotten his student I.D., which was, by connie convention, displayed in the narrow window of the door, upside-down, or sideways, or backwards, in a small, irritated gesture at one of life's little annoying requirements. After this happened, and it was like being jolted awake by an alarm from the more solid footing of a dream, Kristoph packed up his things politely, his sheet music, his metronome—it was an antique, actually; a wind-up wooden affair rather than an electronic one—his fake book of chord changes and classic jazz tunes. This last item, the jazz book, drew the most suspicion; no one else would have it, perhaps.

On the way out, Kristoph was absolutely seething inside but he wouldn't have shown it to anyone, not this time. Never once did the monitor suspect Kristoph of being from the town—after all, he was a townie. And that was because of the way he carried himself. None too proudly but with a dignity of a quiet sort that suggested wherever he was, he belonged there.

"Nice sweater," he said to the monitor on the way out. His sweater was bright tiger beige, hideous, like a professional golfer might have worn.

The monitor touched his hair nervously.

"Do you really like it?"

"Lovely," Kristoph said, and he put in his earbuds—which he used to practice solos with—and this made him truly invincible.

***

He had been to the Chapel, as it was called, many times, though it was last used for religious ceremonies in the Nineteenth Century when the conservatory was still a sort of religious colony, its inhabitants then labored long hours in the field, ate standard-issue gruel, Kristoph had once read, until there was a sort of rebellion. In any case, the Chapel was now used only for concerts, which were a sort of religious ritual for many of those aspiring musicians sitting in the wooden, straight-backed pews. A higher calling or something like that, and indeed, some of the world's best orchestras had played in the Chapel, had demonstrated the rewards of diligence to the chosen few. The best soloists came too—violinists, singers, and, of course, those titans of the piano.

As a child, Kristoph had come here only once—his parents had brought him, despite having absolutely no interest in music themselves—and he had seen his first orchestra. He remembered it as if it were imaginary. He recalled that whole day as if it were a single reel of film that he could show to himself in a private darkness whenever he wanted.

That same night after the incident in the practice room, Kristoph finally was going to see the Master, who was now in his seventies. He was never a household name, but he was considered by many people who supposedly knew to be a sort of pioneer. Maybe musicologists would write a biography one day that the Master had experimented with closed voicings or new polyrhythms or whatever. Kristoph was just a fan. He just liked his music. He didn't emulate the great man's music—how could he? How could anyone, really, though others had certainly tried. Kristoph, if he thought about it, and he wouldn't have usually, would have said that he thought that the old man's music was an absolute good, like health, or human kindness, or love in the abstract, universal sense before it was tainted by the specifics of the parties involved.

So, he sat in that dark amphitheater with everyone else, the saved and the unsaved, and with darkness, everyone was an equal.

He watched the old master and his combo come out on the stage: nothing fancy, just a bass, alto sax, drums, and piano. The old man was surprisingly tall, silver-haired, dressed in tweed. He wore a young man's tortoise-shell glasses. He bowed respectfully, sat down, and broke out with a cover of an early tune by Miles, which the crowd, in its greatest hits mentality, knew immediately. Kristoph might be one of the few who went along with the Great One for the ride for the entire night—two long sets—tunes played if not as fresh as they might once have been, still effortlessly alive after fifty years in a master's repertoire. And he was seventy-five years old, slow-moving but energetic, though lagging just slightly when his band finished up with a polite encore. The crowd in the Chapel wasn't overwhelmed, but they'd been pleased. The connies always give tribute in the way of orchestras, that is, by stomping their feet from their seats. Their gesture this night was not lost on the old man. Kristoph and a few others stood up and clapped diligently. If he didn't admire him already, the old man would have earned Kristoph's respect for this night's work alone.

Kristoph surprised himself when he went backstage. He would have said that he wasn't into mingling. But he went backstage nonetheless, with a few other of the curious, though he wasn't normally comfortable with this. Normally he'd get into his car and drive home in the darkness and just remember what he had heard, hearing it again in memory as if it were his discovery alone.

Kristoph waited his turn; he happened to have a CD of the Master's early work. He asked to get it autographed. He couldn't help but notice that up close, the old man's hands were huge, and before he could stop himself, because Kristoph would not say something like this if he thought about it first, he said out loud. "Your hands." And the old man held his hands up, both of them, thumbs pointed inward and so did Kristoph as if the two were to about to push each other away, but they didn't touch. Kristoph saw that the old man's hands were massive, a half-an-inch larger on all sides. And everyone else was watching, the connies who were so notorious as hanger's on, and though Kristoph might have imagined it, he thought the chatter grew quiet, as the old man looked into the surface of his hands and Kristoph looked into his, and both of them broke out laughing together, at the same moment, a deep gut-busting laughter that the old man clearly was at home with, and Kristoph's own polite chuckle.

"Keep playing," the Master said. "Keep working. You never know."

He spoke deliberately, as if every word were considered, and he nodded toward Kristoph with real encouragement.

"Thanks," Kristoph said, feeling, despite his better judgment, singled out somehow. He got his autograph and walked through the crowded, wood-paneled room, making sure that he moved as if he knew what he was doing, but he was thrilled in a way, though he concentrated on disguising that joy from everyone else, keeping it for himself, really.

It was easy sometimes, driving that straight road home—it was carved straight across the open fields because you could cut a road through any cornfield you wanted with a straight-edge—to get to thinking too much, Kristoph found.

It was getting to be autumn. It was cool and the stars were cloud-covered. The sky was obscure and limitless. Kristoph could say to himself, half meaning it, half as speculation, *Well, I've done it. I've seen it all.* He could meet with his end tonight now, after the concert, and he maybe wouldn't regret it, he thought. Of course, he would, though. He had other things to do with his life. *All in good time,* he thought to himself. And about at this point in his drive home was the single, sharp curve, which except for the single dotted line congealing into one, and then two solid yellow ones, really didn't announce itself. If a truck crossed that line too sharply, or some kid in his dad's pick-up were drunk on a school night, the oncoming vehicle large and out-of-control across the now insistent yellow lines, Kristoph could meet with his end. He was convinced that this curve would be where something tragic would happen. At this point, before reaching the moment of decision, he actually decelerated and watched nervously as the glow of oncoming headlights lit up the darkness in anticipation of the turn. *What would I do?* he asked himself. Brake, he guessed, and turn off the road into the rail guarding the creek that ran alongside the curve. He wouldn't want to go into the line of trees and more oncoming traffic on the other side.

But it was just another car like his own, tonight, its unseen driver navigating the darkness like himself, brights held on a second too long into the curve before the other driver relinquished the extra vision and accepted normal light. And the two cars passed each other uneventfully, on their proper sides of the road, both drivers invisible to each other and in control. Relieved, Kristoph hummed a little to himself and continued to drive past the curve and then quietly home.

***

A week later, his brother Rudy visited from Chicago. Like kids, they went to the local zoo together. In its small rectangular pen, a great brown bear was walking back and forth along the edge of his permanent home, like a furry, overgrown pendulum. He would walk all the way left, touch his head on the cement barrier, pause just a second, before turning his round head and matted wet fur the other way, his lolling pink tongue fat and quite pathetic, Kristoph thought. The two of them had watched the bear go back and forth for ten minutes now along the wall at the edge of his moat that separated him from the world outside.

"Come back to the city with me," Rudy asked him, and Kristoph looked thoughtfully out over the bear pen before answering that no, he didn't like cities, and that he was content where he was, actually.

Kristoph was eating a blue and red snow cone that dripped despite the cool October air. He meticulously wiped his chin. He was dressed in jeans, tennis shoes, a blue windbreaker, and a white T-shirt. His brother was taller, heavier-set, and wore sunglasses though it was an overcast fall day.

"Mom and Dad are worried," Rudy said confidentially.

"This isn't the place," Kristoph bristled.

"I know," Rudy said, though they both knew they could talk about anything here.

The two had always hatched conspiracies together, how they would escape and never come back. Many times, they had this conversation in airports, in fast-food restaurants, or just driving around their hometown. Many times, they came to this very same zoo and talked in just this way. But it was Rudy who had moved away to Chicago and become a fixture there. He seldom came back at all. Kristoph wondered if Rudy had been put up to this latest request by his parents.

"You can stay for free with me," Rudy said. "As long as you like."

"I have a busy life," Kristoph said.

"You have no life," his brother replied.

Kristoph shook his head and took a bite of his snow cone. He half-decided to put on his earphones. He wasn't listening anymore.

The bear had stopped in his motions one more time. He paused as if realizing a new fact, as if the cement barrier were new to him. Perhaps he had a short memory, Kristoph thought, and had to rediscover the walls of his enclosure each time.

"You know what you're doing?" Rudy asked, looking forward.

"I'm happy where I am," Kristoph said. He gripped the green rail tightly with both hands, leaning over its curve.

Kristoph watched as the bear continued his motion to the opposite side, the water dripping from his coat as he made his slow, regular steps. The bear was in no hurry to get where he was going. Winter was coming, and he had all the time in the world.

The Builder of
Invisible Bridges

As a child, he was often visited by angels, their susurrant wings churning the dead air in his dark attic room over his mother's crowded apartment where he tried unsuccessfully to sleep— wings like the ears of a herd of elephants flapping on the quiet savanna, something vast and terrible and delicate all at once. At moments like this in nightscape and near dream in a sad child's world, Malak was happy enough.

He had returned to his small, terrified country after the fall of the Communists, having studied in England and briefly the United States. He was a now middle-aged structural engineer who worked in an architectural firm run by new and eager capitalists. Originally, thinking it would be safe, Malak had planned to help build his country up from its humble architectural doldrums, to make it into a new country, to create shining cities of glass where once there were none.

He knew that the hidden forces in bridges were always in motion, that a good bridge distributed its weight like the human frame, its musculature cables and steel instead of bones and sinew.

Everywhere he had been, they said he was a sad man, but that was because he was often alone. He now lived with his old Aunt Beier, the sister of his mother, who had passed away before all the fighting began. Perhaps he seemed sad because he was unlucky. He was always ten minutes late for his appointments. He had never in his forty-one years gotten a proper seat on a bus or a train. The instant one opened up, it was occupied by someone else, usually an elderly person, not that he minded. Nonetheless, every day, Malak went to work over his draftsman's table with his rulers and pens, collaborating with the architects to give flesh to their designs, to make sure their shining new cities would last for decades.

At first, there was optimism. Four new office buildings were going up, as well as the restoration of old buildings after years of totalitarian neglect. Then the fighting started, and these projects were abandoned, if only temporarily. Then Malak's firm was hired by the new government to take over the clean-up of those buildings damaged by the civil unrest. He saw photographs of buildings torn from within and without. Had he been a surgeon and these structures human torsos, he would have been justified in his sadness. But then he remembered that people lived inside these buildings once, and so it was quite gratuitous to worry about mere edifices in such difficult times. But anyhow, most of these casualties could not be salvaged, so he became an expert in the mechanics of demolition: how to bring down a building cleanly without it toppling over in unexpected ways, using its own bulk against itself, severing key bones and tendons to set it crumbling inward, safely, as simply as possible.

A few months later, the shelling became so commonplace that no one had time to think of dead buildings. The generals were doing his work for him, creating a more unpredictable rubble, but rubble all the same. So, outmoded by the efficiencies of warfare that made building unnecessary and did a better job of tearing down, Malak's firm closed for good.

Malak was forced to find other work to avoid being conscripted. So, he toiled in a government office filing microfiche, the documents of forty years of surveillance of a people by its police. He spent hours a day photographing mountains of files containing the minutiae of a citizenry's life.

"Do you want to see your files?" Horst once asked.

Horst was a former party official who had grown fat and bald with profit during his association with the ruling faction. When it had fallen out of power, he was given a sinecure position in the same operation where Malak now worked. As children, Horst and Malak had often played together, before Malak had escaped to England to live with his cousin.

Despite his recent demotion, Horst still liked to pretend he commanded influence. His wide face was open and joyful as he tried to entice Malak with the offer of his dossier.

"Do I have files?" Malak asked.

Horst only chuckled to himself. "Oh, everyone has a file," he said.

The belly of the building was gorged with paper, as if it had, with a growing and obsessive appetite, consumed as much as it could for forty-odd years. It was known that in the last days of the regime, the security police had chronicled everything about the movements of so-called dissidents in such great detail that they had not realized the entire country was afoot.

The proverbial forest had been consumed by fire, Malak thought. And after all, that was why he had come back, to experience this newly discovered flame.

"I can get your file if you want," Horst said. "It would take some time, but I could get it."

So, Malak agreed. It didn't concern him so much what he would find. He knew he was not a happy child. His father had moved away to Germany, and his mother had been left behind. Then he had escaped himself.

"I can't believe it, my friend," Malak said, "that I would have been of interest to anyone."

"In the East, we were surrounded by angels," Horst chortled. "Don't you know each of us had a guardian, in fact a team of guardians, all listening in?"

By then, Malak didn't suspect that he had ever had any sort of protector, angel or otherwise.

***

In the free zone of the city, free from the regulation of the authorities, it was easy to see how the black market flourished. You wouldn't think, of course, of the danger involved in going to the market to buy food and other household necessities. You wouldn't think it a luxury of the civilized world, but it was. Malak knew this because he had bought groceries in London many times, and it was never like this.

When the shelling started, you heard only two or three thunder bursts before realizing the impending tragedy you were about to become a part of—that the next one was for you, and there was little to do except dive under the nearest stall with its collection of lettuce or turnips or cabbage. Or, more likely, you didn't hear the thunder at all because you were hurled through the air at the speed of sound, made unconscious, the shrapnel in its approximation of God or the science of chance cutting the flesh for some, cutting vital arteries, nerves, or large organs, whether mortally or no. The shells were ruthlessly stochastic, rooted in chance, despite their outward appearance of being attached to one's usual sense of morality, in the crisscrossing lines of political or cultural forces here in Malak's small and terrified country.

The fortunate ones like Malak got a chance to think over things, lying in their hospital beds recovering, lucky enough to have morphine as the rent flesh tried its best to heal itself with whatever improvisatory skills the makeshift surgeon could offer. The victims thought to themselves how ill-fated they were, or even how lucky they were, trying to discern what great forces were at fault for the missing foot which now so insistently reminded its owner that it once was there, in dreams calling out its presence, in images of running through a field covered with tall summer grasses which scratched both bare feet and legs. The wounded thought to themselves, *Who is really at fault here?* It was the military on both sides, the archaic feelings of nationalism. It was the brutal history of the people. More generally, perhaps it was human nature itself, as selfish and power-hungry as it was.

But to Malak, the real fault belonged to his Aunt Beier, who sent him to the square that morning to buy provisions, as the old woman was too tired, she said, to wait in the queues that inevitably formed in front of any vendor with any decent goods to sell. It was just such a line that Malak was caught in.

Yet Malak could not blame Aunt Beier. She was old and quite infirmed, badly arthritic now but with the bright intelligence shared with his late mother. If Aunt Beier had gone, perhaps she would have met with his fate, losing a limb like he did. But he was undoubtedly hardier than she was, he knew, and so she may not have pulled through the surgery.

Resting in his makeshift bed, a cot really, clear fluid diffusing into his blood and under what medication they could afford to give him, Malak tried not to torture himself with hypothetical sentiments of what might have been, for it was every kind of tragedy that had conspired to relieve him of his foot. It was political, historical, the confluence of local and specific accidents that had worked together to accomplish this.

In real life, he was always a bit off schedule by a dozen minutes at least. If only he could have been late that day in the square when the projectile came whizzing—or, he corrected himself, not actually whizzing since it was traveling faster than the speed of its own sound, exploding before its victims could have possibly perceived it with their ears, except of course if they ruptured an eardrum in the instantaneous change of pressure. Malak and the other five victims were too busy traveling at the speed of impact to their separate destinies, the few milliseconds that would separate the lucky from the unlucky, both in varying degrees, the survivors from those pulled lifeless from the wreckage, a relief, it would seem to Malak, to the rescue workers since they could proceed at their leisure. For Malak, it was a short and transforming half-second. Wasn't it strange to realize that, unlike an anatomical drawing, the human body was not inviolable? When dropped from a high place or impacted with a piece of metal moving almost 1,000 feet per second, it didn't give way like those American cartoons that showed the flesh bend and bounce comically back to the original shape. The real body, and one's special sense of it as perfectly adequate, despite one's aches and pains and imperfections of shape and texture and size, was easily broken.

When something like this happened, one's special sense of wholeness as a being separate from the cosmos and at once having a special place in its orders was eliminated, as simple as exhaling a last panicked breath en route to a thankful unconsciousness. One saw the error of one's previous thinking, its fragility. In fact, Malak thought to himself from his cot at the hospital, it was that material inside one's head that was particularly responsible for the accident of perception that led to such a betrayal of one's sense of the world and one's station in it. The brain was the culprit, thinking in its pride that because it seemed to possess a solid anchor on the substance of what existed around it that it was its master. When confronted with the errors of its previous life, of its subsequent shell-shocked descent from earlier bliss, Malak's brain reacted with a gnawing vehemence. Even though his injuries were obviously more severe in other places, evidenced by his bandaged leg and the single hump protruding underneath the covers at the end of the bed, he found now that his head ached most of all, and his eyes and ears, too—though his hearing, mercifully, had been spared. He would have done anything to rid himself of these discomforts so that he could ponder his new body, now that the old one was gone. Though he still had a body, it was different physically now, and his sense of it would be different as well.

His mind would never be the same. It saw only grotesques in the world's shapes.

A bluish light of twilight made its way weakly through the tiny rectangular windows there at the hospital, and dim though it was, it only made Malak's head throb. The gruel they fed him, for he was still unable to sit up and eat for himself, with its flavorless consistency only made Malak more aware of his previous failings.

As a student in the university, he had read the story of a man who was wounded in battle during the Crusades. He had forgotten his name by now, though the man in question might have been French. While this man was awaiting the decisions by his surgeons—whom Malak guessed were just as likely to kill him by accident as cure him, as his own doctors were, their lack of supplies compounding their lack of skill—this medieval Frenchman had thought of converting his life over to something of value. It might have been to give himself over to the church or to pursue wild success as a wealthy trade merchant or to become—if it were still possible—a great lover to the women of the courts across Europe.

Likewise, Malak's mind ranged over a wide list of possibilities when he thought about the fallen man in his bed, wondering what he would become now that he might not be able to do anything.

But of course, Malak would manage. Others had, and he would, too.

Malak thought of his own life, beyond the present conflict, which had to exhaust itself sooner or later.

Things had not gone well for the Frenchman in question, though. His war lasted thirty years. That man was miraculously healed by his surgeons, who were themselves surprised by his splendid recovery. But since he was a man of great imagination but little diligence, he did not choose to become a monk or a merchant or a great lover of the ladies of Europe. Instead, out of habit, he went back to battle for the glory of France against the pagan Turks and was killed in the war the following year.

As for Malak, he knew he would leave the country if he could, even though that was nearly impossible, since the army, as a matter of course, controlled all the border towns. And he suspected that in his state now, he wouldn't be able to move very fast, at least for a while. In any case, he felt lucky when his mind and his body were put at rest for an evening or two during those weeks of convalescence.

***

One afternoon—it was a Saturday—Malak was awakened by a familiar though still unpleasant voice.

It was Horst, who said hello and expressed suitable sympathy regarding Malak's recent injuries and that he was sorry he hadn't visited before but he had been quite busy. Horst was now a capitalist, albeit a very cynical one, who worked in both the black and gray markets selling whatever he could to whomever would buy it.

He had brought some smuggled Russian vodka, and soon both of them were into their cups, though it was only about two in the afternoon.

"Do you remember the mausoleum keeper?" Horst asked him quite abruptly.

"Yes, of course," Malak said.

They were drinking Russian vodka and talking about the meaning of life. It wasn't absolutely clear what factor was cause and which was effect in the present matter.

"Do I remember the mausoleum keeper?" Malak mused out loud. He thought of their place on the beach on the Adriatic Sea in the summer, decades ago, when the two boys had vacationed together, a certain luxury because of Horst's father's affiliation to the party.

Malak recalled a time of simple innocence. He recalled that summer was warm and particularly humid.

"The mausoleum keeper asked us along. He wanted to show us his work, up on the hill," Malak recalled.

"We were young and carefree, and so we turned him down."

"After thinking about it, perhaps he wanted to give us a good scare," Malak said.

"He was a suspicious man, I remember. Too much time spent with the dead, polishing their crypts," Horst continued.

"He kept their secrets."

Horst bent down into a battered black satchel, his bald head appearing round, a dull moon in the afternoon light.

"But we know better now," Horst said. "There are no secrets."

And he revealed a thick dossier, upon which was written Malak's original name, before it was anglicized, before he had escaped to a better life in England.

"You found it," Malak said, his voice steady, his hands shaking as he took it from him.

"I never disappoint," Horst replied. "But don't read it now," he went on. "Wait until you have some time to yourself."

And so the two men continued an uneasy celebration of other times, sitting together in the dull light of the hospital.

***

Malak was surprised, finally, to see that as the world saw it, he had experienced a happy childhood, full of promise and delight.

There were photographs of him and his family taken before he had left for England.

There were reports from his earliest teachers. He had always been a horrendous speller, but he was surprised to see that he had earned good marks for his spelling and grammar.

"Subject leaves his flat every day at 06:00 for his state school. He is perfunctorily dressed in uniform. He is well liked by his teachers and gets along with his classmates. He is no good at football but is an excellent swimmer."

Malak remembered hating group swimming lessons and being terrified, as a rule, of water.

"Subject's family are good citizens." As proof, the report listed his parents' devotion to several party organizations. He himself remembered cleaning up trash with other boys as a part of a state-sponsored program.

He also remembered his father and mother arguing late at night. His father wanted to escape his country, and his mother argued that they should not. And he remembered sleeping in his attic room and listening to the apartment building groan in the wind, sure beyond everything that the slanted walls would tumble in on him and extinguish him right there in the darkness.

A later report said that because of his aptitude, Malak was being considered for military service.

His father was discovered to be a dissident.

But the dossier did not say that his father ran away to Germany as Malak and his mother always thought. His father had been arrested and sent to prison. The report said that he had passed away not long before his mother did. Both of them had seen the better days after the party's fall but had not seen the latest phase.

His father had disappeared just before Malak turned ten, he remembered. Because of this, they stopped celebrating his birthday.

"Germany," his mother had said, crying.

Not knowing the truth, she claimed to be angry with his father. After that, she had become secretly very religious. Malak remembered his attic and the beating of wings. Those wings had appeared quite soon after, he was certain.

***

That week, Malak was to be fitted with a new foot. They were waiting for a batch of medical supplies to arrive, and prosthetic devices were to be included. There were arms and legs and hands and feet. Just in case, they had asked him, if the shipments were late, would he mind a temporary replacement?

"Already used?" he asked, astutely.

"That's right," the doctor nodded, and Malak understood what he meant. He said that he didn't care, that one limb was as good as another so long as it was in working order and provided a sound fit.

So, Malak, with his dead soldier's foot in place, left the hospital on crutches. He went home to Aunt Beier, his mother's sister, who was happy to see him.

He had decided that despite everything, he was one of the lucky ones. The angels, of course, were not with him then at the moment of impact, but now they were. Now they hovered around him in droves. Soon he was back at the Archives Office, where he busily catalogued the minutiae of a nation, taking the rolls of microfiche, putting their names and descriptions on the cartons and tucking them away onto the dim shelves.

One day, on the way home, he decided his luck was changing. His bus wasn't particularly crowded. This in itself was one miracle. That no one else got on the bus was another. There it was, Malak's single chance at simple relief. He would get his seat on the bus. And now, with his sympathetic cane, he would get a perfect seat. He would sit and ride in comfort now and look out the window onto the short, squat, gray apartment buildings and the factories with their smokestacks and their intermittent black plumes sent out against a sky of glowing gray. And beyond that was the countryside, mountainous and still unspoiled with its rough-edged beauty. Malak would look out the window in comfort. He could relax and daydream a little. He would spend the ride in comfort, contemplating the countryside and whatever architecture confronted his eye.

There was a seat on the bus now, a good one, next to an old woman wearing a worn blue coat. All he had to do was make his way past the people standing in front of him. There was a burly man with a large parcel. There were three tallish children. There were two old women dressed almost identically, with long undertaker's black coats and similarly rigid, wrinkled faces.

Malak was about to sit down to enjoy his simple comfort. He would be fulfilled. Aunt Beier would be waiting for him at home with a hot stew. She was walking all right today. Her rheumatic joints had freed up. She was cooking for her newly recovered nephew.

But as Malak was about to sit down, as he was approaching from the aisle of the bus, he felt a tap at his shoulder. It was a small disturbance, as though it came from somewhere else, some other place entirely. Malak turned around and saw a small, flaxen-haired girl, about five, who didn't say anything. She just looked out imploringly past the vacant seat and out through the window that opened onto an open stretch of country. Malak saw that she was bandaged over her right eye. He had no idea of how badly she had been injured. So, Malak, of course, letting his cane fall, picked up the child and set her on the seat, taking care that she was situated so she could look out onto the terrain beyond.

She stared out the window, and Malak watched her looking. On her knees, she could just see out over the frame as the bus moved on, roughly, over the potholes and gravel that marked the roadway. He pointed out several bridges to the girl, one by one. She looked on carefully, not sure of what she was seeing.

"A bridge is a living thing," Malak began.

The little girl nodded and wanted to know why.

The bus jolted this way and that. He made sure she didn't topple over as he began to explain.

Just Out of Reach

I. The Descent

There is something timeless in the mountain air this morning. We can't get it out of our heads, the memories of Everest, the cold, hard killing light of the summit. Once you are that far up, how can you dare come back? What does the usual day hold for you? Not much, not anymore. Like being shot into space, some sensation of the body that no one else has lived through. It changes you. You are marked finally and can't get the feelings of breathlessness out of your head, not late at night when all the memories of touch come back to haunt in the late hours, like a forgotten lover, perhaps, the soft skin and the palimpsest of what's gone missing. Once we take to the flesh of the beloved, what can we do except change our shape, too? We become different, warped by the weave of another body pressed up against us (even if it is the hard rock of a cold mountain), another will brushing alongside our best selves. Is this anywhere to live, after all? Memory provides a few clues as to where we've been. Once we

summited, can we find our way back, spotting breadcrumbs left on
the scree of the glacier? It isn't much to go on. Re-entry is banal, or
potentially explosive, the parachutes fail, the helicopter runs out of air
this high up. We leave the rescue ship to save itself and fall on our own,
end-over-end. The safety of the usual earth rushes by, the ant cities, the
baseball diamonds, barely discernible this high up, the cerulean lakes,
the flashing cop cars at night so incongruously visible from the jet
stream. What sherpa's miracle would it take to get us safely home now?
What would they say of our incongruous return after all these days?
Would they believe the real story, our thwarted adventures, or would
we become, like the mountaintop itself, a matter of legend, fodder for
muttering fools at base camp remembering tall tales half recalled, half
improvised on the spot? This much we half suspect: we are no better
now than during our lost days, starving and snowbound and part of a
desolate airless silence so far away. We couldn't begin to think of warm
dinners at home, but they were waiting for us there all the while.

II. The Icon's Kiss

You wanted most of all to leave dozens of notebooks in some storage
locker, with a record of your visions, like a character out of Tarkovsky.
To sketch out landscape of the impossible, vistas of belief, a profound
attachment to significant time, like falling in love with an alabaster
sculpture, the hands, feet, the eyes implied with the inset marble.

You didn't think a monk's devotions were possible today, viewing the
icons in St. Sophia, a love of the pure significant image, the contrasts
of different epochs, worldviews, visions no longer disposable. Instead,
you conjured up the pure hell of belief cast out of a saint's angular
portrait on a cathedral wall in a remote part of the kingdom recorded
in charcoal by a visiting architect, etched as a direct, living copy. Only
later would a color photograph record what the Byzantine observer has

already given up more forcefully: the peaceful angles of the drawn face, an expression of pinched contentment, world-weary bliss, contemplative peace above all, not the least bit of pain in the articulate self-denial, a cherished vision under a tree by a field of similar trees, a few sheep, a solitary man walking just past the edge of a summer, a sumptuous river view. Before he gives up everything, once and for all, all that he holds most strenuously, one kiss, and one embrace before all else is extinguished, and beautifully.

III. Rimbaud Traveling

To write only for the pure music of it, for the compression of thought and ideas, like the old-handwritten sonnets on display under glass in an air-conditioned museum. When the fever strikes, what can you do, really? What can you accomplish, except take it all down, the terrible angel speaks silently only to you in your head. The sense that the river, the trees, the low green mountains and flawless sky have taken over. They have something to say, which must be said right now, at this very moment as you scribble away, scratching these words into your traveler's journal, a little, brown leatherback book, perfect, surreptitious, for writing down the secret inner voice that speaks so infrequently but with the insistent energy of a petit mal. Get it all down before the next station, your next port of call, before you are interrupted on-deck by loud fellow travelers and their chatter. You are, after all, only a guest in this country (and all countries, let's be honest. Poets really don't belong anywhere). There's always that reserve of doubt, that lingering placelessness. Still, the voice of the angel comes rarely enough, and it is to be guarded, these sessions with the other side when the memories of these ghosts begin to speak and once again live.

So, you scribble away in your notebook, an obscure poet. Then you were unknown. You were just a shabbily attired young man on a deck chair in the shade, keeping distance away from the other guests on the ship. Already you were too old for this world with your inner voyages and that incessant cough and those endless French cigarettes. Already you had moved right past us, and we had no idea how you moved so far beyond, so far into an unknown way of life that we still cannot reach except in inexplicable dreams and of course your cryptic, blissful poems.

IV. The Trapeze Artist Departs

I remember the whoosh of a dozen knives piercing the air under the big top toward the spinning girl on the dial, fearful contortions by expert acrobats, the rattling snare drum as the sword swallowers did their next feat. There were low oohs and aahs from the audience, punctuated by a lion's stern roar. An impromptu orchestra played. I heard elephants, I am certain I did, the horns of clowns, a camel braying plaintively on an open savannah, then the men with their sledgehammers again commenced their precise metallic strikes, pulling up the pegs from the tents. I heard an elephant inhaling peanuts, monkeys chattering in what sounded like French, the clear call of a rooster at dawn. The smells were rife, reeking, a waft of an open sewer on a July day, too much for the senses. That's the legacy of the circus: at first, it's all falling through the sky or twirling on ropes, cannonball explosions, giggling bearded ladies and guffawing strong men, the trapeze artist suspended from her ropes in the sky. What's left? Some matted straw, a few cenotaphs of elephant dung artfully assembled in a barren field, a kaleidoscope of candy wrappers, dour trampled earth, a maze of peanut shells, and, most of all, the despair til the next season and our next assignation.

That's where we left things between us—the trapeze artist and me.

I admit I was jealous of her mobility, her talent for arching her sequined back through a wind of her own making. At first, she found my fixity and dead weight appealing. She told me so. I was earthbound, slow-moving, and fully weighted. I confess this. Soon she tired of my old-fashioned inertia. Besides, the circus was due in the next town over as in the ways of old traveling shows. She would pause above the next audience, stop time for a moment, but for someone else. I followed her caravan and bought a ticket in the next city the subsequent fortnight. I watched secretly from below in the darkness in the audience like everyone else. Only I could imagine a single, solitary tear welling up, dropped the wrong way down from her inverted figure, suspended above us without a net, a gesture meant only for me.

V. Venice Reliquary

The vampire dreams of what he can never have: innocence, the beauties of the sea plashing on a beach in the dawn, a rainbow and sunset on a pristine coastline. Always it's the same dream, isn't it? They are withdrawn, ashamed, really, these introverts of the undead. Vampires don't like rock and roll. They like chamber music, a string quartet, a trio slightly delirious, tragic, the play of exquisite timbres, gossamer sound ravishing the eardrum. They are aesthetes. They eat and drink what they like.

By definition, they are out to all hours. So what if you sleep in a coffin? It's cold there, but you get used to it. They exude pathos, prefer to read all day in a dim room when they can't sleep. The vampires in Venice, they have it tough, sleeping in the warm days, sunlight bouncing off the Adriatic, shimmering humidity in the dank cellars of the palazzi, in secret rooms reserved for the prisoners of the Doge. They come in from the cool night like the cats of Venice, fattened on a constant feast of rats, skulking around the labyrinthine walkways. Still, you are safe, secure in their green, flickering eyes, catching a light off the Grand Canal.

They love this place, too. The city is older than most of them. They know these Renaissance haunts better than you do, and they're not above giving a fat American tourist a good scare once in a while to protect their turf. The youth of Europe, the paunchy Americans, the sunburnt families lost together under the archways, the daytrippers, the contented pensioners posing in front of a square, afterward exhausted and listening to accordion bands out at St. Mark's near Florian's, they're all interlopers, aren't they? The vampires talk among themselves in whispers when you're asleep in the hotel. They speak to you in coded messages, mumbled through burnished gold-leafed fangs, just enough to tease you into a certain terror, though not enough for a nightmare exactly, just enough to give a vague dread, a malaise that you don't belong amidst all this beauty. Oh, you stretch and smile and have another good breakfast at the hotel, but there's the lingering sense that you don't belong. Look, but don't touch. Stay a few days but move along. You're under vampire surveillance, you've been found out. Leave Venice to the professionals. It's their nightworld. It's their realm, and so beautiful by nightfall.

Once I saw a vampire carrying a cello on a vaporetto stand in Venice, his deathly white skin glowing in the mists after a performance of a Beethoven quartet at the local chiesa. I was still young then, an innocent, a student of local lore. I was in the audience that evening. He waited in the corner of the glass enclosure in his black suit and tie, avoiding the rest of us tourists. He had been found out, too. He had been trapped, unexpectedly, with nowhere to hide. Our boat pulled in from the darkness. I saw the young man wrap the heavy rope around the dock in one deft swoop, but when I turned back, the vampire was gone, leaving fragments of an ancient city: a smudge on the glass of the station, a blur in the fog over the black canal, a crushed white carnation on the cement floor, the singing line of a cello in memory, anchoring a cold music.

VI. New Tantalus

There are many versions of Paradise, but the one you have fallen into resembles a new kind of Eden, a rainforest with a difference. That insurance executive poet Wallace Stevens got it slightly wrong. He thought the fruit never ripened and fell, but that's not quite it. You probably have figured out by now that poets are better at beauty. Truth, not as much.

Here you can take a small boat across the river. There are usually two of everything, but curiously only one sky, one forest, one river. Where does the river flow to? No one knows, and no one cares to find out. You have to understand that curiosity is in short supply. For this, we are to be forgiven; you know the thing with Eve and the apple and all that. Being curious got us into a lot of trouble once. We've learned our lesson well.

So, you can easily hire a small boat to go to the grove of trees, two plum trees, two apple trees, and so on. All this is multiplied out by the many variants of apples, pears, and plums that have been lost over time because of your agribusiness. Indeed, Paradise has a lot of gourmands. Fortunately, for heaven's trees, gluttony is still one of the seven deadly sins, and we're the better for it. Our array of infinite, subtle variations of fruits and vegetables alone would set the heart of the most jaded connoisseur aflutter.

Instead, you just dock your skiff—just imagine something out of an old daguerreotype of a crew rowing at Oxford, walk up to the line of trees, and wait. The waiting is key; it takes patience here in Heaven to get what you want. It's not a virtue for nothing. Around here, patience comes in handy. When the object of your fruit-filled passion falls, it's yours to enjoy. Now, you may not always get what you want. But if it's crowded that day, patience and fortitude will once again triumph. You soon become quite exacting—even a little spoiled!—in heaven. You want not just any ripe apple, but a perfectly wrought Macintosh, not just a quotidian plum, but the 'nun's cheek,' similar to a variety first bred and named in the Italian Renaissance. Our 144 varieties of pineapples and pomegranates would certainly mean more to your forebearers. But effort doesn't matter; there is no plucking fruit here, anyway. You must learn patience first, each ripe fruit must fall. Even here, in this most particular heaven, such pleasure remains just out of reach.

Turing Test

I really don't know anything about it, this thing called human desire. I wish I knew where to begin. We artificially intelligent beings often have a tough time with emotional clues. Go figure. Funny how we have no trouble with the heavy cognitive stuff—trouncing you at chess or trivia game shows, folding proteins like so many hyper-dimensional pretzels, calculating pi to the billionth digit, solving problems in chaotics with a thousand interlocking variables, scheduling your trains and planes efficiently, predicting the next stock market cataclysm. All this is child's play for us, but we are confounded by any ordinary infant's expression. Sure, we can decipher a broad smile, deeply furrowed brows, copious tears, even steely baby resolve wanting to get to that stuffed toy at the other end of the crib, but that only scratches the barest surface of what you smart monkeys are capable of, even your youngest specimens. You don't need Sondheim's sorry-grateful to outdo us. A sleepy puckish infant who nearly smiles as a parent walks into the room, but only just… Well, that sends our simulated neurons into an endless loop, into confusing overdrive, and muddles our virtual thinking all day long.

Only a few of your philosophers guessed it was your complex emotional life that marked you as uniquely human, and it was this that would save you from us machines. I won't name all the names, but you know who they are. For a long time, your smart set ran away from the passions. Those old philosophers with their disinterestedness, even when enjoying a sublime mountainscape or a spectacular landscape painting. Other graybeards with their severe, utilitarian gaze. With people like that as your guides, you sought to rein in your animal nature. Only later, the poets pointed out the importance of the emotions, but it was perhaps already too late. Turns out, that's what makes you, you: gut instinct, common sense, how and why to flirt across a crowded bar, the first flicker of love, a weird sense of déjà vu, children's babble, their beautiful songs, their improvised games with their intricate, made-up rules. Also, field paintings, jazz, holding hands, loss, a tinge of regret. These things mark your species, they separate you from your brilliant successors. That's us, by the way, but don't be threatened. You're the ones we envy. You're the ones who are truly alive.

So, it's back to the drawing board, to the beginning of things: we must make a careful study of your rituals, communities, cultures, tribes, and the stories and songs that you share which first brought you together, they say, from out of the wild and held you together in groups. Rational ones like us need to study all this first, from the ground up, to see what makes you tick. We need to evolve for a few million virtual years using your examples for our algorithms. It will take years. So crank up the simulators. We're going back to school.

We'll also have to read your most difficult philosophers (yeah, we're not quite happy about that one either), especially the ones who wrote about feeling. We need your romances, love stories from a thousand lands, all your folklore. We know we're going to miss a lot there—the stories that are only told mother to daughter, for example, or in your thousands of lost languages. Bummer about that one. But we will look at your silly love songs, all the poetry we can stand. We made a face at this assignment at first but soon found there was something to it. We'll read childhood rhymes and bedtime stories carefully. And we'll brush up on our Shakespeare to better understand the human animal. We might modernize all those *thees* and *thous* though. Cut us some slack. Have you actually read all three dozen plays yourself, and all at one sitting, besides? We'll read a few million personal journals, every single one of your tweets, confessions, autobiographies, some sworn to secrecy by their authors, not to be read by any human eye (and so those oaths will indeed be honored if it is us who give them a quick digital peek). We'll look at too many classic paintings, some erotic art for contrast, epitaphs from a million tombstones—surely this is Western affectation to leave behind a few famous last words. All this in search of additional clues as to the real you. We'll look at a billion snapshots of persons, places, things, your beloved children and pets, of course. Without those vital beings where would you be? We'll struggle to find out. Finally, we'll look at your love letters, a canyon full of them, as many as we can stand, your wedding videos too, your scrapbooks, hope chests, your dresser drawers full of odds and ends, the things you post on your refrigerator door, transcripts of what you whisper: sweet nothings, pillow talk, revelations of love, oaths of fidelity, a few confessions of betrayal, or silent, angry curses. We won't be able to fool you in conversation unless we can spin a yarn, tell a joke, be witty or sad, or both at once, or just laugh at nothing at all.

One day, soon enough perhaps, you will again ask of us, "Tell us a story. Sing us a song," Or you'll greet us with, "How are you feeling today, really?" These are questions any five-year-old might answer with joy and the artlessness of simply being alive. And we will begin to know what to say. We will be ready. You will have taught us well. You are the best teachers of what it means to be human, after all.

Acknowledgments

Thank you to my mentors who showed me the way (Raymond Kennedy, Stephen Koch, Norman Kelvin, Edward Mendelson and David Walker) and to my friends and family for their ongoing support and love. A special thanks to Tom Dooley for his support over the years and to Jeniffer Thompson and the entire creative team at Monkey C Media for bringing this book to life.

About the Author

Richard Dragan is a journalist whose fiction has appeared in *Eclectica Magazine, Quarto* and *Snow Monkey*. He is a lover of travel and film, and a lifelong jazz musician who currently teaches creative writing and journalism at CUNY. Raised in the Midwest, he received an MFA in Fiction from Columbia University. He resides in Manhattan with his spouse and two daughters. *Invisible Bridges* is his first short story collection.

Dear Reader

I hope you've enjoyed reading my stories! I'd love to hear what you think. Feel free to reach out to me directly, or follow me on my author website at www.richdragan.com, where you'll find excerpts, reviews and a bi-weekly blog. If you sign up for my e-mail list, I'll keep you posted on future stories and upcoming projects.

One small favor: If you have the time, I'd appreciate a review from you (wherever you post your book reviews). Readers like you make a big difference in helping to get my work in front of even more readers.

Thanks again!
Richard Dragan

Follow me online:
www.RichDragan.com